Jean Jambon

Our Trip to Blunderland

Or, Grand Excursion to Blundertown and back

Jean Jambon

Our Trip to Blunderland
Or, Grand Excursion to Blundertown and back

ISBN/EAN: 9783337139148

Printed in Europe, USA, Canada, Australia, Japan

Cover: Foto ©Andreas Hilbeck / pixelio.de

More available books at **www.hansebooks.com**

OUR TRIP

TO

BLUNDERLAND

OR

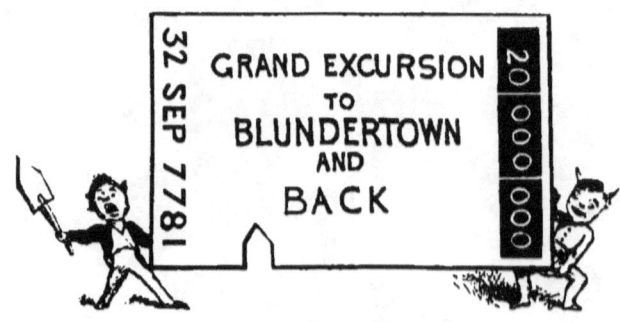

GRAND EXCURSION TO BLUNDERTOWN AND BACK

32 SEP 7781

20 000 000

BY

JEAN JAMBON

WITH SIXTY ILLUSTRATIONS BY

CHARLES DOYLE

THIRD THOUSAND

WILLIAM BLACKWOOD AND SONS
EDINBURGH AND LONDON
MDCCCLXXVII

THE NURSERY HAS ITS SHARE OF MY DAY, IN SUCH FASHION THAT LITTLE PEOPLE MAY NOT THINK BIG PEOPLE CREATED TO STOP FUN AND TO BE A THROTTLE-VALVE ON ANIMAL SPIRITS. BUT THERE ARE ROMPS AND ROMPS, SOME BEING BEYOND AN ADIPOSE SIX-FOOT-TWO. HENCE THIS STORY. PERHAPS IT WILL PROVE ACCEPTABLE AT COOLING TIMES IN OTHER NURSERIES, AS IT WAS IN OURS.

IT MAY BE THOUGHT THAT IN INTRODUCING A CERTAIN LITTLE LADY ALICE NCE HAS BEEN TAKEN. BUT ROYAL PERSONAGES ARE PUBLIC PROPERTY. WILL HE THAT CROWNED QUEEN ALICE DEIGN TO ACCEPT THE TWO LITTLE PAGES DEVOTED TO HER AS PROOF THAT IT IS HELD AN HONOUR TO FOLLOW IN THE TRAIN OF CARROLLUS PRIMUS? FORBID IT THAT THIS ONE SHOULD LOSE HIS HEAD, OR BE FACILE, EXCEPT IN CONJUNCTION WITH PRINCEPS. LONG LIVE CARROLLUS LE WIS! FOR IF HE FAILED US, WHO COULD BE GOT IN LIEU IS A QUESTION. NEVER WAS THERE ONE GREATER AT THE FEAT OF PUTTING THINGS ON A CHILD'S FOOTING, AND TO HAVE BUT HALF HIS UNDERSTANDING OF HOW TO DO IT IS THE SOLE AMBITION OF ONE

JAMBE ON.

OUR TRIP TO BLUNDERLAND

GRAND EXCURSION
TO
BLUNDERTOWN
AND BACK

little boys (whose names you must not know
—so, choosing something like them, thёy shall

be called Norval, Jaques, and Ranulf) had been reading all about Alice, and the strange, funny things she saw and did when fast asleep.

"I wonder," said Jaques, "if I could ever get to sleep like her, so as to walk through looking-glasses, and that sort of thing, without breaking them or coming up against the wall!"

"Oh," said Ranulf, "wouldn't it be nice if we could! only the funniest thing is how she got through the wall. I don't see how being asleep would help her to do that."

Norval, the eldest, broke in—"Oh, you big stupid! she didn't go through it; she only thought she did."

"Well, then," said Jaques, "I want to think it too. Last night when I was in bed I tried to go to sleep, and to get through the wall; but when I fell asleep I forgot all about it, and dreamed that I was sick, and that the doctor gave me a big glass of something horrid."

"Ah, but," said Norval, "that was because you tried. Alice didn't try, you know. She knew nothing about being asleep till she woke up."

" Well, I didn't know I was asleep till I woke up, either," answered Jaques.

Ranulf looked very wise, although he was the smallest, and said, " Perhaps if Alice was here, she would tell us how to do it."

" Of course I would," said a sweet voice behind them ; and, turning round, who should they see but little Alice herself, looking exactly as she does on page 35, where she is getting her thimble from the Dodo ?

" Oh, how awfully jolly !" cried Norval ; " will you help us ?" He was very much surprised, not at seeing Alice, but at not being surprised.

" Indeed I will," said she, " although I don't know, you know, whether boys can manage it."

Ranulf was just going to say, saucily, " A great deal better than girls, I should think," when Norval, who was older, and knew better how to behave, checked him, and said—

" But, Alice, dear, surely if it's done by going to sleep, boys can do that as well as girls."

"Well, so they can," said she; "but then, you see, everybody who goes to sleep doesn't get to Wonderland."

" Oh, but perhaps," said Jaques, " if you will go to sleep too, you will come with us, and show us the way."

" Ah! I can't do that to-day," said Alice, looking very grave; "for, you see, when I came to you I was just going to give Dollys their dinner —such a nice dinner! cake and currants; and it would be cruel to leave them looking at it till I came back."

Now Norval suddenly remembered that he knew some boys whose uncle was a Director at the Aquarium, and who, when he could not go with them and pass them in himself, gave them a written order; so, turning to Alice, he said—

" Oh, but if you would give us a pass, it might help us." And sitting down at the writing-table, he wrote in stiff letters, imitating the papers he had seen, and laying the pass before her, said, " Now, write ' Alice' there ever so big, and put a grand whirly stroke under it."

Alice obeyed, and the pass was ready.

" Now then," said she, " you had better go to sleep."

Norval threw himself down on a sofa ; Jaques and Ranulf coiled themselves up on the rug.

Norval could not resist the temptation to keep one eye half open, that he might see what Alice did. But she, noticing this, held up her little forefinger, and said, "Come, come, that won't do." Thus rebuked, Norval shut his other eye.

" Now, all go to sleep at once," said Alice.

" I'm nearly asleep already," said Jaques.

" Oh !" said Norval.

" No !" said Ranulf.

" That's talking, not going to sleep," said Alice.

All was still for a little, then Jaques half uncoiled himself and looked at Ranulf.

Ranulf uncoiled himself and looked at Norval.

Norval raised his head, and looked at Jaques.

On finding that they were all awake, the three burst out laughing.

" That's laughing, not going to sleep," said Alice.

Down they all flopped again, and then Alice, to help them, said, " Hushaby baby, on the tree-top !"

" I'm not a baby," said Ranulf, much offended, as he was nearly six.

" I'm not on a tree-top," said Jaques.

" You've waked me up," said Norval.

" That's chattering, not going to sleep," said Alice.

" I'm sure I must be asleep now," said Norval.

" So am I," said Jaques.

" And me too," said Ranulf.

" That's talking nonsense, not going to sleep," said she. " I see it's no use; Alice's way won't do with wild rogues like you, and I really must go back to Dollys."

" What *are* we to do ?" said Norval; "we can't fall asleep. Don't you think we could get to the funny places you went to without going to sleep?"

" Will you do what I tell you ?" asked Alice, holding up her little forefinger in a dignified kind of way.

Jaques had some misgivings about compromising his position as a small lord of the creation by agreeing to do what a little girl told him; but his anxiety to see some wonders prevailed, and they all said that they would obey.

" Shut your eyes, then, and don't open them till I tell you, and perhaps something will happen."

Norval rolled down from the sofa to the side of his brothers. Then all squeezed up their eyes quite tight, and although they heard a curious rumbling noise, did not open them.

"That's right," said Alice; "you would have spoiled everything if you had peeped. Boys who don't do what they are told spoil everything, and themselves besides. Now you may look!"

They had squeezed their eyes so tight that it took ever so long to get them unfastened. Jaques got his open first, and saw that little Alice was gone.

"Oh, Alice, where are you?" he cried.

A distant voice replied, "Off to Dollys!"

Just as he was going to say, "What a shame, when I squeezed so hard!" Norval and Ranulf got their eyes open, and before Jaques could speak, they gave a wild shout, "Hurrah! hurrah! hurrah!" Jaques' head had been looking the wrong way, but when he turned round he saw what the others had seen—

THREE BICYCLES,

only they were ra-
ther different from
other bicycles, as,
in place of the small
hind - wheels, there
were funny little fel-
lows, made up of a
head and three legs;
and as they stood
on one foot, with the
other two in the air,
and their noses thrust

through the end of the bar, they looked very comical. Still more funny was it when the boys went forward to look closer, and the little three-legged men made them a bow, which they did by touching their caps with one leg, bobbing forward on another, and back again. The wheels and treddles were made of gold, the seats were lined with crimson velvet, and the little men had blue tights and silver caps and shoes; so everything looked very smart. The boys could not understand how the bicycles stood upright without anything to hold the wheels, and began talking about them, wondering whether they could move of themselves. They had scarcely spoken of this, when, as if to show off their powers, the little men began to turn round on their three legs, and move slowly about the room. They steered their way among the furniture most cleverly, and at last as each stopped beside one of the boys they all touched their caps, and bobbed from one leg to another, as before.

"Are we to get up?" said Jaques, timidly.

Bob went all the little men.

"Does that mean yes?" said Norval.

Bob.

"But where are we going?" said Ranulf.

"To Wonderland, of course," said Jaques.

"All right," said the other two, and they all scrambled up on the bicycles.

The moment they were seated, the three little men gave a shrill whistle, as a railway engine does before it starts, and off they went at a tremendous pace. The boys had barely time to think how hard the drawing-room wall would be, when the whole party went straight through it as if it had been, like circus hoops, filled in with paper. Norval went across the library and out at the window, but papa did not seem to notice him; he only got up and closed the sash, as if he had felt a draught. Jaques passed through the butler's pantry, but the butler only scratched his ear, as if something had tickled him. Ranulf shot at a slant through the nursery, clutching a penny trumpet off the table as he passed, but nurse only gave a shiver, and said, " Deary me, I do feel so queasy queer!"

They were going so fast, that Norval, looking round the moment they were outside the house, saw papa's head, not bigger than a black pin's, looking out of a window, that seemed smaller than a halfpenny stamp; and Jaques caught sight of Oscar, the house dog, who looked like a comma with its tail wagging.   Besides, they kept mounting up in the air as well as going on, so that the fields looked no bigger than the squares of a chess-board, and the trees between them, in their autumn tints, like rows of brass nails on a green-baize door.   Before they could count fifty, the world itself, when they looked back, was like one of those funny worsted balls that show a number of different colours.   The little men were spinning so fast that their silver caps, blue hose, and bright shoes ran into circles, till they looked like silver wheels with a blue enamel ring on them.

" Isn't it funny that we aren't frightened?" said Jaques.

" I think we would be if we had time," said Norval (who was the thinking one of the three), " only we are going so fast that there's no time to be frightened."

" Perhaps it's because we're asleep like Alice, after all," said Ranulf, looking very wise.

" Oh no; because you see when people are asleep they are still, and we are going so fast that it would be sure to wake us," replied Jaques.

" But we can be still and go fast all the same, can't we ?" said Ranulf.

" Oh no, you silly !" said Jaques.

" Oh yes," said Ranulf; " because we can go still faster ; and if we can go still faster, why can't we go still fast ?"

" Oh yes, to be sure," said Jaques; "and besides, of course, a man can be fast and still at the same time, for if he is made fast with rope he must be still."

" And we *are* going fast still," said Norval, as the bicycles flew on; "but I don't see yet how we can be still and fast both."

The three seemed likely to get into a regular muddle about this, when their attention was suddenly called off by Jaques catching sight of something that looked first like a new threepenny-piece, and in another second like a big shining tin plate.

"What's that?" said Jaques. While he was saying this, it had grown as big as a drum.

"Perhaps it's a giant's dish," said Ranulf. It was now as big as a circus.

"It's getting too big for that," said Jaques. By this time it was as large as a race-course, and in another second it was too great to be like anything.

Norval, who had been thinking, was just going to say, "Perhaps it's the moon," when the Man in the Moon put his head out at one side, and looking as grumpy as possible, called out—"Hi, you rascals! what do you want here?" He had evidently been wakened out of a nap by the whirr of the bicycles, for he wore a big red nightcap, and had got only one eye open.

"We aren't rascals," said Jaques; "if you say that, we'll tell papa."

"Oh," said Norval, "are you the fellow that came down too soon?"

Ranulf broke in—"I think you've got up too soon this morning. By the bye, did you ever find the way to Norwich?"

The Man in the Moon got quite red with rage at this, opened his other eye, and aimed a blow at Ranulf with a big stick.

"Ha!" said Jaques, "that's one of the sticks you gathered on Sunday, you villain!"

As his arm made the blow, it came nearer the boys; and the stick, which had looked only like a porridge-stick, got as big as Nelson's Monument. Ranulf would have been knocked to pieces, but the little man at the back of the bicycle gave a sudden dart to one side; the Man in the Moon overbalanced himself, and if his wife had not caught him by the legs he would have tumbled off the moon altogether. In struggling to get on again his red nightcap fell off, and a breeze of wind carrying it away, left it sticking on one of the moon's horns.

They were now getting so near the moon that they began to wonder how they were to pass it.

" Jump over, to be sure," said Jaques.

" Oh, that would be a tremendous jump!" replied Ranulf.

" Not at all," said Norval; "you know the cow jumped over the moon, so it can't be very difficult after all."

The bicycles began to move a little slower, and the boys thought they were going to stop, but it turned out that the little men were only gathering themselves together, like good hunters, for the spring; for in a moment they gave a whistle, as a train does when it goes into a tunnel, and the bicycles bounding up, went right over the top of the moon, the boys keeping their seats in a way that it would be well if some Members of Parliament could imitate.

As they passed, the Man in the Moon, who had come up after his nightcap, shouted, " Don't you come here again!" and picked up a stone as big as four hayricks to throw after them. But before he could do so, his wife, who had come behind him, and who had a nose as big as

a ship's long-boat, eyes like paddle-boxes, and a
mouth like the entrance of a harbour, seized him
by the arm, boxed his ears, and said in a voice
loud enough to be heard hundreds of miles off—

" Would you hurt the dear little things, you old
villain ? "

" Old villain ! 'ld villain ! villain ! 'illain ! 'lain !
'lan ! ln ! " cried the echoes in the stars.

The Man in the Moon dropped the big stone on
his own toes, and muttering, " Petticoat govern-
ment again ! " pulled his nightcap over his ears,
shrugged his shoulders, and went home meekly
to breakfast.

" I wonder if we're going the same way the cow
went ! " said Ranulf; " if we are, perhaps we may
get a drink of milk—I'm so thirsty."

" And a beefsteak," said Jaques ; " for I'm
hungry."

" Faugh ! " said Norval ; " what would papa
say if he heard of our eating cow-beef in Fairyland ? and as for milk, if she runs as fast as we do,
she must be run dry long ago."

The pace was now greater than ever, so that the stars flew past them like sparks from a smith's anvil. They had been going through darkness for some time, when they perceived a dim light in front; and soon they saw that it was a grey cloud, into which the bicycles plunged, moving more slowly, till they came to a walk. While they were in the cloud, the boys felt that they had come to ground; and in a minute or two they passed through it, and found themselves in a very bleak, cold-l oking place—no grass, no trees, no flowers, nothing but stones and sand, and an old woman walking in front of them, thick fog enveloping all round. Ranulf was almost going to cry, it looked so dreary; but Norval told him to remember that papa often said, "Whatever happens, don't cry, but be brave boys; things are always made worse by crying." So he gave three big gulps and was all right. But they began to think in themselves that if they had known Fairyland was like this, they would have preferred to stay at home. They had little time to reflect,

however, for the old
woman tripped her foot
against a stone and fell
down on her nose, which
was very long.   The
boys jumped at once
to the ground, forget-

ting all about Fairyland, and rushed to the old woman to help her up.

"Poor granny!" said Jaques, "are you very much hurt?"

"Verily muchly," said she, in a squeaky voice, that sounded like the noise which a piece of paper stuck over a comb makes.

It was so funny that they all felt inclined to have a laugh; but they kept it down, and helped the old lady up. Her nose was so long that their handkerchiefs were too small to tie it up, so they fastened them together and bandaged it as well as they could. They were going back to the bicycles, when she said—

"Don't go away, dears."

Norval said, "We wanted to get on to the nice part of Fairyland, but if you would like us to stay till you feel better, we will."

"Yes, of course we will," said Jaques; "won't we, Ranny?" And Ranulf gave a big nod.

Then the old lady, patting Ranulf on the head, replied, "You want to get to the nice part of

Fairyland? So you shall, for those who are kind are sure to get what is nice and pleasant at the proper time." While speaking, she seemed to get enveloped in a kind of mist, through which the boys could only trace her figure dimly. To their great surprise, the fog that was all round and above them began to weave into lines; and these plaited themselves together quickly, till they formed a vast trellised dome. Then light began to break through, and the dark bars became transparent gold. Lovely plants rose from the top of the dome, twining themselves in and out all the way down. Each had hundreds of buds, which, as they reached the ground, burst into leaves and flowers in dense profusion—here a thread of blue, here of red, here of white, which, mingling with the golden trellis, produced a charming effect. The ground, which had been rough and stony, smoothed itself into stripes of silver sand. The stones became precious ones of all colours, and ranged themselves along the stripes of silver, making beautiful, shining walks. In the plots

between the walks, the most lovely grass appeared,
soft and delicate, like velvet; and from each
there rose a crystal fountain, playing waters of
different bright colours; while all around richly
laden fruit-trees sprang up, with many splen-
did-coloured birds on the branches, which began
to fly in all directions, whistling and singing
most sweetly. All this time the mist remained
round the old woman, only turning to a beautiful
rose colour. When the fountains and trees were
rising, the boys gazed in wonder and delight.
Ranulf proposed to pluck some fruit and eat it,
but Norval said they must not do that without
leave. Presently the rose-coloured mist began
to get thin, and, clearing away, they saw a beautiful form appearing—a regular real fairy, standing perfectly still in the middle of the canopy,
shining so bright that though everything else was
beautiful, she was the loveliest of all, as she stood
in the midst of a bouquet of flowers formed of glittering jewels. For there was a bright shining in
her face that outshone all else—a something so

beaming, so winning, so unlike anything to be
seen in the world of every day, that you must just
try to think of what cannot be thought of, before
you will get any idea of it. Her robe was dazzling
white, and the swan-like neck and rounded arms
vied in delicate beauty with the strings of gorgeous pearls that formed the only sleeves of
her shining dress. The slender waist was circled
by a band of glittering precious stones, and her
skirt, falling to the knee, was one blaze of silver
light, the fringe at the edge sparkling with bril-
liants. A tiara of diamonds crowned her head,
and lovely golden hair hung below her waist.

Jaques' mouth and eyes opened wide, and
Ranulf showed two large dimples in his cheeks
as these wonders came to view. Norval was the
first to remember what he was about, and said,
" Come along, boys; we must go and shake
hands, you know, and say, How do you do?"
So they all went forward. As they came near,
a lovely smile broke over the fairy's face, and
she held out her hand, saying, " I am so glad to

see you, dear boys; and still more to see that you know how to behave like little gentlemen." Her voice was clear as a silver bell, and her hand very curious to touch, but so nice. She went on, as she stooped down and smoothed Ranulf's hair, " You will see every day the advantage of being good and brave. Do you know what would have happened if you had not helped me, when I was the old woman ?"

" Oh, but you couldn't be the old woman," said Ranulf, looking up admiringly in her face.

" Indeed I was, dear," said she; " I just wanted to see whether you were unselfish, kind boys, so made myself very ugly and ridiculous. But do you know what would have happened if you had not picked me up ? "

" No-o-o-o," said they all, shaking their heads.

" My servants would have whirled you back faster than you came, and dropped you on the rug again."

" What servants do you mean, please ? " said Jaques; " we didn't see any."

"I will show you," said the fairy, giving a light bound to the ground, and walking across towards the bicycles, which were modestly standing at one side of the bower. She had shoes of transparent glass, with buckles of lovely sapphire; but what astonished the boys most was, that the glass was not stiff, but obeyed the movement of her beautiful feet, so that her motion was splendid, the foot curving gracefully down as she stepped, reminding the boys of one of the large stately-moving birds they had seen at the Zoological Gardens. They gazed at her in amazement, as she smoothly glided; and she, observing their surprise, said, smiling—

"So you admire my shoes. I get them from the same man who supplied my sister fairy with those she gave to Cinderella. He's the very best maker in Fairyland."

As she came near the bicycles, the little men made their bow as they had done to the boys, and then raising themselves off the ground, whisked round two or three times in the air, as if in great delight. The fairy tapped each of them with her wand, and at once they became handsome pages, older and bigger than Norval, dressed in dark-blue doublets and velvet caps, with pretty ruffs round their necks that looked transparent like glass; and, with their light-blue tights and silver shoes, they were very smart. Each stood leaning on the great gold wheel, which was all that remained of the bycycles.

" Oh," said Jaques, "we didn't know they were real; we half thought they were only funny machines like men,"—and turning to the other boys, added, " Must not we say 'Thank you' to them for all their trouble ?"

" Of course," said Norval; and each went up to his own page, and said, " Thank you very much."

" That's right," said the fairy; and the pages smiled and made a bow—just an ordinary bow, not whirling round as they had done before, for, of course, pages cannot turn over of themselves.

" And now you must be hungry, dears, after your long journey," said the fairy, giving a graceful wave of her hand towards the three pages. In an instant they were down on one knee with the golden wheels supported on their heads, like three lovely Dresden-china art tables, while their caps, which they tossed on the ground, grew and shaped themselves into silver stools. And how it came about the boys never could make out, but there was a neat little dinner laid out on the top of each wheel; and still more curious, each boy had his own favourite dish, only nicer to look at and better to taste than they had ever had it before. While they feasted, low strains of music sounded sweetly through the air, and a chorus of many voices, clear as the crystal brook, but gentle as its murmur, sang *—

I.

"Boys of earth, be brave, be true,
        Linger not at vice's call;
Cords of love are drawing you,
        Chains that guide but not enthral.

* *Air*—" Silver Threads among the Gold."

Break them not, their fragile lines
  Draw with strength the willing heart
To the life that ever shines;
  Angels weep to see them part.

2.

Let the cords of love entwine
  Round the heart-strings day by day;
Let the threads of silver shine,
  Guiding by the narrow way.
Watch, lest thorns of pleasure's bower
  Tangle in their tender strands;
Guard, lest Mammon's subtle power,
  Fray and loose their gentle bands.

3.

Worldling's life is love's decay,
  Pleasure's slave hath joyless end;
Squander not life's fleeting day
  In the paths that downward tend.
Follow truth and yield to love,
  Bravely keep the narrow way;
Truth shall greet you from above,
  Love shall bring to endless day.

4.

Truth and love endure for aye,
  Silver love in truth shall hide,
Golden truth for love doth stay—
  Truth the bridegroom, love the bride;

Sun's strong beam to moon's soft ray,
   Truth and mercy met in one,
Blend in everlasting day,
   And again the work is done."

When the boys had dined, which they did with exceptional ease, as their knives and forks did not require to be handled, but performed their work neatly and deftly of themselves; and when the table-napkins had unfolded themselves, and touched their lips with deliciously scented water, the last strains of the song died away; and the fairy, who had herself sung the final verse in tones most winning, so that the boys had crept close to her, nestling under the caress of her arms, stooped down and kissed them tenderly.

"And now," said she, "I know you want some fun, and quite right too. Those who go steadily in the right road are well entitled to a little diversion, and can enjoy it better than the boys who choose crooked paths. Now, where would you like to go?"

"Oh," said Norval, "we have a pass from Alice to let us into Wonderland."

"Ah! Alice; I have heard of her, or rather I've heard her. She was the little girl that grew so big, was she not?"

"Yes."

"Well, when she got big, her voice got big too, and it was heard all over Fairyland."

"But are there more places than one in your country?" asked Norval.

"Oh yes, dear, of course there are; we have Elfland, and Bogieland, and Spriteland, and Wonderland, and Blunderland, and many others. But let me see your pass."

Norval produced it from his pocket.

"Why," said the fairy, "this is not for Wonderland; it's for Blunderland."

And so it was, beyond all doubt, as may be seen by looking at this copy, faithfully and literally taken from the original writing :—

"Oh, how stupid!" said Norval. "When I was writing it I said to myself, I will try not to make any blunder in spelling; and I must have written Blunder from thinking of it. What are we to do?"

"Never mind," said the fairy; "there is plenty of good fun to be got in Blunderland, and you may just as well go there as anywhere else. So now good-bye, and I hope you will enjoy your-selves."

Once more the lovely hand was waved—this time the arm in its graceful curve taking in every part of the palace of gold and flowers—when in-

stantly a thou-
sand fairies
stood in one
vast circle a-
round, and
gracefully
bent low be-
fore their

queen. Then with a bound each took her place
opposite one of the trellises of the bower, standing with the right foot pointed, and waited for the
signal to begin the dance.

The queen, with many a graceful turn, circled
round the glittering ring of dazzling fairy brightness, waving one hand outwards to this fairy and
the other inwards to that ; and though there were
a thousand of them, and she thus, in soft floating
dance, went round all, yet it seemed to be done
almost in the time that the eye could follow her ;
then with a bound she once more stood in the
centre of the great bouquet, and having slowly
drooped in a deep long curtsey, acknowledging
the reverence of her subjects, sprang to her full
height on tiptoe, and threw her hand above her
head, holding a rose that she had worn at her
breast, which burst out into the form of a star,
scintillating with light of most dazzling brilliancy.
This was the signal,—and in a moment, ching,
ching, ching, ringa, ringa, ring, went the million
little silver bells upon the skirts of the fairies, as

they floated in graceful measure hand in hand. Then each laying hold on one of the supports of the dome, they raised it up, and danced round, carrying the canopy with all its myriads of flowers with them, faster and ever faster, till the eye could scarce follow the ever-shifting shades of dazzling colour,—the light from the queen's hand, varying ever and anon, changing the whole scene from dazzling brightness to crimson glow, from green gold of sunset to soft purple of fading twilight.

The boys stood gazing in mute wonder and delight at the graceful motion of the queen and her fairies, having never seen any dancing but at a ball at home, where people rushed about, elbows meeting ribs, and strips of tulle and tarlatan torn and scattered about; or at a spectacle, where a pantomime fairy seemed trying to jerk off her shoes.

Presently the rapid thrilling ching-a-ring of the bells — through whose chiming a melody not to be described, but wonderful in its sweetness, caught the ear — became slower, the fairies to whom the queen had waved her hand outwards turned round, facing those to whom she had waved inwards; and out and in they glided, ever faster and faster, the trellis-work of the canopy unplaiting as they went, till the last crossing being undone, the fairies ranged themselves on opposite sides, the bars making one long, brilliant, golden-arched bower, the end of which seemed small in the far distance. Then the queen, with a merry smile that had something half-roguish in it, kissed her hand once more to the boys, saying—

" REMEMBER !

BRAVE AND TRUE ; "

and before they had time to think what was going to happen, the bouquet shaped itself into a magnificent chariot, the three golden wheels set themselves one in front and one at each side, the pages sprang up behind, and gliding like a flash down the golden bower, the chariot was lost to view.

The boys were just going to set off running after it, when a tremendous

WHEEEEEEU$_{UUUUUU\text{-}}$UGH

sounded from an approaching train, the station bell rang close to their ears, and a gruff voice above them shouted, "Train for Whackbury, Flogland, Dunbrown, Sillybilly, and Blundertown." Not that it sounded like this, for it was spoken precisely as on all railways at home, and sounded just

"Train frwabryflugglindenbrunnsilblunblurtun."

But that matters as little on fairy railroads as elsewhere. When the boys looked up they saw that the voice came from a policeman, about as tall as a three-storey house, and no thicker than a Maypole, standing with his arms sticking straight out, and who had an extra eye to safety, blazing red, both in front and at the back of his head. Just as they looked up, one arm

flopped down to a slant, and an eye winked funnily from red to green, so that he was a caution to look at. The train now appeared dashing out of the tunnel (golden and bright no lon-

ger), going so fast that the boys thought

it must pass the station, and were horrified when they saw the porters busily throwing down a quantity of black things like two-foot-long tadpoles on to the rails, and then, a little further on, a big, round, black ball.

" What's that for ? " said Jaques.

" Well, them's stops. We goes about as fast as thought, so we checks and pulls our trains up the same way as they do trains of thought, with commas and colons."

And sure enough the train, after crashing through the commas, came to a stand just as two funny little buffers, whose heads stuck out in front of the engine, seemed on the point of being black-balled by the full stop. It is true that the commas seemed not to be placed with any care, but just dropped down on the lines anyhow ; still in this the system varied in no way from the mode in which commas are scattered about the lines of other great works as well as railways. In fact it seems to be the rule, that commas come as they like ; and if they come upside down they can bring any amount of material to one work from another — a new proof that one of the greatest powers of the age is commars.

As the train came to a standstill, the policeman's eye winked suddenly back from green to red, and his arm flew up again, while he shouted—

"Smash'll, smash'll, smash'll."

"Change furcrotnchipucklgublboranquklin ;"

by which he meant, "Change for Crowtown, Cheepcackle, Gobbleboro', and Quackland."

The boys' attention was called to the engine, by the station-master coming up in a rage to the driver, and stamping his foot on the ground, shouting, "Here's the ninth day this week that you have come in punctually, when you know that it is against the rules. You must have a blowing up."

"All right, sir," said the driver, meekly ; and mounting the engine, he quietly took his seat upon the safety-valve.

The boys, who had bought a little steam-engine

with the savings of pocket-money carefully hoarded for many months, knew something of the

danger of this proceeding from the printed directions sent with their engine, and Norval cried out, "Oh, don't do that, or there will be a burst!"

"All right, little un," said the driver, "it'll get me hup in the world."

As he spoke he was shot into the air as high as the tall policeman's head, and the boys shut their eyes in horror, thinking he must be killed. But on opening them again, to their surprise they saw him at his post, quietly buttering a piece of bread with wheel-grease, and taking a drink out of the engine's oil-can.

"Are you not hurt?" asked Jaques, anxiously.

"Yes, 'urt in my feelin's. It's wery 'ard hafter getting so 'igh to have to come down to this agin; but we must take things has they comes or goes, has the man said when 'is 'ead flew hoff on bein' axed to do so."

The engine did not appear to be more damaged than the driver by the explosion, and on looking at it, the boys were surprised to see that its boiler was shaped like a porridge-pot, with an immense porridge-stick stirring it by steam. There was a tender behind, which kept the engine up; for, as the driver said, in answer to one of the boys, "We keeps 'im coaled to keep 'im ot. My hengine begins to 'eat up when 'ee's swallered two tons. In fact it's with this coal 'ere that 'is bile is riz." *

"And what have you got in the pot?" asked Ranulf.

* The words, "Till 'ee gits it he's coal as a cokeumber," are in-

The driver, who had just taken another pull at the oil-can, so long and full that the fireman had to beg him to leave some for the wheels, replied, 'Don't ye ax souperfluous questions." But the fireman, picking up a big spoon like a warming-pan, plunged it into the pot, and held it down to Ranulf, saying, " There, you'll find that 'ere souperfine stuff."

" It ain't 'are soup at all," said the driver ; " what are yer talkin' about ? "

" That's just as well," said Norval, " because one can't live on air, of course."

" I dunno that," said the driver ; " jugged 'are's wery good stuff for dinner."

" Oh, but," said Jaques, gravely, " if we got nothing but a jug of air for dinner we would be just full of wind."

He thought to himself, just as he said this, that perhaps this was the right thing for a driver of a

terpolated in the MSS. ; but doubts of their authenticity, and fears of ruptured sides in the case of those who might think a joke was intended, make it prudent to delete them.—ED.

puff-puff, as they called railway-engines in the
nursery, but he did not like to say so.

After Ranulf had tasted the soup, Norval and
Jaques had some, just as the porter came along
the train calling out, " All tickets for soup ready,
please; tickets reade-e-e-e.   All tickets for soup
ready, please."

" But we haven't got any tickets," said Ranulf.

" Then," said the porter, "where's your fare ? "

" Well, we had fairy fare a little ago."

" But I mean railway fare," said the porter.

" Oh," said Norval, "we've just had it too,
and first-class fare it was ; at least it was fair
fare."

" All right," said the porter ; "but any boy who
travels without his fare, or his ticket for soup,
will be breeched for breach of the company's pie-
laws, remember that."

He tried to look very fierce as he said this ;
but as his body looked like a barrel, with three
big X's upon it, and his head was a large pew-
ter-pot, the boys could not help laughing, which

Norval excused by saying, "I beg your pardon, but you do look so dumpy."

"In coorse I does," said he. "Porters no good that bean't stout, you know."

"Oh, but you're so stout!" said Jaques.

"No, I ain't So's stout," said he; "I'm Dublin stout."

" If you're doubling stout," said Norval, "that's as stout as can be, isn't it ? "

" No, it ain't. I'm more than that already. Don't you know treble X when you see him ? "

" Oh yes, I know now," said Jaques. " I've heard papa say that X is an unknown quantity; and you're three times him, are you ? "

The porter was off by this time at the door of a carriage, looking at tickets, so he gave no answer; and the boys' attention was called off by the passengers that were changing for Crowtown, Cheepcackle, Gobbleboro', and Quackland coming along the platform to cross the line. First came Sir T. Urkey, of Gobbleboro' Hall, in a white hat, a red handkerchief sticking out from below it, a brown coat, and tight leggings. Next followed Mr Shanty Cleary, his wife Henny, and half-a-dozen little cheeps of the old block following. Mr Shanty Cleary's head presented a most combical appearance, and all the young Clearys of the male gender took after their father in this respect. Last came M. U. S.

Covy Drayck, Esq., the tails of whose coat curled up in a very funny way, and who carried his head very high, as if the whole country belonged to him, although he was rather bandy-legged and very flat-footed. He seemed altogether inclined to play the swell; and as they passed the boys, bobbed his head to one of the Miss Clearys, and said, " Oh you little duck ! "

" Duck yourself," said Mrs Cleary, with a most indignant sweep of her head; " my daughter's no duck, Mr Imperence." Mr Shanty Cleary himself stepped forward, with his head as high as he could ; and looking as cocky as possible, was just opening his mouth to say something severe, when Sir T. Urkey turned back and said, " What's the matter ? "

" He's giving my chick cheek," said old Cleary.

" He's trying to crow over me," said Mr Covy Drayck.

" Come, Drayck, don't be a goose," said Sir T., "and behave yourself. You're no chicken now, you know."

"Who asked you to interfere?" said the other, throwing back his neck as far as it would go, and waddling up to Sir T. in a most defiant manner.

Sir T. got purple in the face, and swelled out under his brown coat with rage, his red handkerchief slipping loose, and a long end of it hanging over his nose, nearly to his waist. He rushed at Mr Drayck, with his coat-flaps trailing on the ground, and tried to speak, but nothing came out except a gub-gubba-gubble-gubble-gubble.

Mrs Cleary, seeing there would be a fight, screamed out, "Police! police!" as loud as she could. The tall policeman gave a horrible wink, showing the white of his eye, at which signal two other constables seized the ill-behaved Mr Drayck by the neck, and began to drag him to the engine.

"What do you mean, you rascals?" said Mr Drayck.

"Means to pot you for breach of the pie-laws."

"Where's your warrant?" said Mr Drayck.

"Our pots is all Warrens," said a constable, as they chucked him in.

"There," said he, "you can commit breach of the peas in there if you like; they won't split on you, for they're all split already."

"Take your seats," shouted the guard (who had a whistle instead of a nose, and a big turnip fastened to his belt to tell the time by), as he ran up to the boys, "and mind you don't get in right side first."

"Why?" said Jaques.

"Because if you gits in right side afore, you're sure to be left behind."

The boys went along the platform to look for a carriage. The first they came to had a crown of a hat nailed on its side, and below in large letters—

'ERE *V. R.* AGAIN.

Looking in they saw a king in a long robe, standing before a number of square holes (over each of which there was a letter of the alphabet), with an armful of letters, which he was cramming into the different holes. The H's seemed to be very troublesome, for they were constantly getting dropped, and those that he managed to force into their place the boys saw slyly slipping out, and gliding into the holes of the vowels, so that, struggle as he might, he could not get them right. Once he caught an H with a corner of an I, just as it was trying to get in beside the O's.

"Oh ho!" said he, "is that what you're after?" seizing him firmly. But the H was determined, if he could not be where he ought not, that he would be dropped; and as the king held on tightly to him, over they both rolled together, the king tripping on his long robes, and coming down in a most undignified position. The H's that were on the ground could do nothing, but those that had got in beside the vowels shouted with laughter.

" Ha, ha, ha!" came from A pigeon-hole.

" Hee, hee, hee!" from E.

" Ho, ho, ho!" from O.

Those that had got in beside the I's laughed in a Hi key. The H's that were in the U pigeon-hole alone remained silent, as they could only have called out Heu, which, as it means alas! they were not in the Humour to use.

The king made no attempt to rise, and looked as if he was much the worse of the drop he had had, and in great need of a Pick-me-up; so Norval put his foot on the step to get in and help him, but the king, observing his intention, waved his hand and said majestically—

" Royal Male.

no admittance."

It was evident, however, that he was in great distress, for he called out "Oh!" several times, only the boys could not understand why he put other letters before it, so that it sounded like, "g. p. oh! g. p. oh! g. p. oh!"

"Get out of the way," said a voice behind them; and a gorgeous officer, but who, strangely enough, wore canvas bags, and the orders on whose breast were money-orders, stepped in beside the Royal Male.

"Who's that?" asked Jaques.

"That's General Pustoffus; we calls him G. P. O. for short; it's him as looks after the Royal Male. He's a queer sorter chap he is, the Royal Male. He takes up 'is 'ole time a pullin' letters out of bags, and shoving 'em into 'oles; and when's he's tired o' that, he takes them out of 'oles and shoves 'em into bags. And, besides that, there's never a letter he gets that he doesn't give the Queen's 'ead a bang."

"What a shame!" said Ranulf.

"Ay, it be a shame," said the guard. "If you or me was to lick our wife we'd get six months; but this 'ere Royal Male, he doesn't mind 'er 'ead gettin' licked and stuck fast in a corner, and 'ee's always a stamping on it, and making her face all black. And I'm sure a patienter lady never was, for though her 'ead's being bumped all day, she never says a word. He don't hold the Queen's 'ead worth more nor a penny to a hounce, he don't. But come on, or the train will be hoff."

The next was the smoking-carriage, and the smoke was pushing out so hard at the door, that the moment the handle was turned it flew open, so that it took the united efforts of the guard and porter to get it shut again, the cloud coming out as thick as gutta percha. Norval looked through the window, and saw a pig puffing away at an enormous cigar.

"What a bore! It's no use trying to go in there," said he.

"I thought papa said smoking was a bad habit," said Ranulf.

"Well," said the porter, "ain't 'ee trying to cure hisself?"

" I'd ha' thought," said the guard, " that amount
of smoking would ha' cured him already."

The pig, hearing the
talk, opened the window
and handed out a slice
of himself on a plate,
saying, as
he did
so,

" There, you see yourselves I am not half
cured yet, so don't bother me any more. What
can't be cured must be endured." He gave such

a puff of smoke as he said this, that Ranulf
sneezed a loud " H-a-a-a-m."

" No, I am not ham," said the pig.

" Bacon, then," said Jaques.

" So I do mean to bake on," said the pig, " in
the smoke here, and when I am ham I'll let you
know; so don't take it for grunted till I tell
you."

He shut the window again.

" Why can't he talk correct, and say ' When I
ham 'am' ? " said the guard, as the pig closed
the window.

The next carriage was empty ; and no wonder—
for it was the sleeping-carriage, and was snoring
so loud that even the wooden sleepers below
wouldn't stay quiet, and were anything but chary
of their raillery. When Jaques looked in it only
spoke in its sleep, and said, " Are we far from
Wakefield yet ? "

" Very far, I should think," replied Jaques.

They all laughed at this; and unfortunately
the guard, in laughing, let his whistle-nose go off.

This made the driver start the train; just as the pig opened the window of the smoking-carriage again, and handed out another slice, saying, "A rasher individual than this pig would have made his eggsit as a cure at once, but you see I'm no'* a ham yet; steady's the word for a perfect cure."

This long speech gave time for a tremendous cloud of smoke to escape, so that the train got out of the station under cover of it, before the guard or the porter knew that it was off.

" 'Ere's a go!" said the porter.

" It's more like there's a go," replied Norval.

" Yes, there's a go, and here's a stay," said the guard. "We must get on somehow. What shall we do?"

" Ax old Sammy Fore, 'ee's your man," said the porter, pointing to the signal policeman.

" Vy, vot could 'ee do?"

" 'Ee? 'ee's the very man for movin' people on,

---

* This pig must have been north of the Tweed, to forget his Tees thus.—ED.

yer knows ; 'ee'l be hable to run yer in to the train yet."

They all hurried across to the policeman, and begged him to take them on.

" Do you see anything green in my eye ? " said he.

" Sometimes," said Jaques, " when you wink."

" Then you won't this time," said he. " Don't you know that I'm a fixed signal ? If I were to leave here, I shouldn't be found when I was wanted."

" Just like other policemen," said the guard, " so that wouldn't make no difference. Come, don't be a fool ; take us on."

" Couldn't we go by special train ? " said Norval, who was by way of being very knowing about railways.

" Special train be blowed ! " said the guard ; " let's go by special constable. We'll soon hovertake the train by p'liceman Xpress."

" No, you shan't," said the policeman ; " I sticks to my beat."

" If you sticks so hard, you'll grow to the spot,
said the guard, sulkily.

" Then I'll be a beetroot," said the policeman.

" So you are, with your red and green."

The policeman seemed determined not to help
them, when the guard at last said, in desperation,
" If anything happens to that 'ere train, it'll be a
pretty kettle of fish, for there's a Cooke's excursion in it."

" Cooks and fish!" shouted the policeman;
"why didn't you say so before ?   If there's cooks
in the train, I'm your man.   Come on; cooks
without followers is no good; let's after 'em
at once."

So saying, he whipped up Jaques and Ranulf
under one arm, and Norval under the other, and
bidding the guard hold on by his coat-tails,
started off after the train.   His long legs went
over the ground at a tremendous pace, and as
they flew by, the people in the houses rushed out
to behold the sight of a policeman running, for
they are generally slow enough, as everybody

knows. One old ploughman scratched his head as they sped past, and muttered, " A've offen 'eard as how p'licemen's never in an 'urry, but that un goes like an 'urricane, he do."

" Yes," said another old man, " police rates are as slow as they're heavy generally."

When they had gone several miles in as many seconds, the policeman caught sight of the train, and rushed on faster than ever. But suddenly he gave a terrible yell of pain ; and no wonder—for he had bumped his shin against a bridge crossing the line, which he had not noticed, as he was watching the train. He staggered, blundered on a few strides of 300 yards each, and at last fell heavily forward, and his head went bang through the van of the train, which had come to a stand-still, driving it all the way to the next station, which was about half a mile off. When the policeman fell, the little fellows ran great risk of coming to smash ; but at the back of the train there happened to be two obliging buffers, who, as the shock of the fall made the policeman's

arms fly up, caught the boys, and with the aid
of one or two back springs, brought them safely
to the ground.

"Thou'st roon thyself in this time, lad," said
the guard; "it be looky for oi that I warn't in
the van, or there 'ud a been two brakes in it
instead of one."

The policeman vouchsafed no reply, but
gathered himself up with a most dignified air.
One of his red eyes looked rather the worse for
his tumble; but being a glass one, it did not
matter much, as it could be easily replaced. He
stuck his arms straight out once more, and said,
majestically, "Move on, there!"

The guard being anxious to get to the train,
needed no further urging, but set off with the
boys for the station. After a little, he got so
out of breath that his nose was beginning to
whistle again, and he had to hold it for the rest of
the way, lest it should cause the train to start off
without them once more.

The boys, going forward to get into a carriage,

found the people all jammed up by large pieces of pasteboard, like the advertising placards carried by two men in the streets, which turned out to be tickets. They could not be got out at the doors without a great deal of bending and squeezing and struggling, which tore and broke them ; and as the officials insisted on carefully pasting up each ticket as it was got out, the collecting promised to be a very long affair.

" Why are the tickets so big ? " said Jaques to the station-master, who had used up a paste-pot as large as a drum. They had a paste-pump in the station that was kept constantly going, like a battery.

" Well, you see, my little man," said he, " people were always losing the small tickets, so we thought they would take care of big ones ; and we have not had any mistakes since."

" But doesn't it take a long time ? " said Norval.

" Well, ye-e-e-ss. We generally take about three hours and a half to get things square,—I mean the tickets, for they makes a sad hash of them getting them out ; but then things is square when we've done, you see, and that's the great point."

Norval, who was beginning mathematics, wondered how a point could be great, and how a square could be a point ; but he did not like to trouble the station-master, as he was so busy with the tickets, which, when they were all mended and collected, made a pile that blocked up half of the station.

A number of Sillybilly people came to the station to get into the train for Blundertown. It was already so full that the boys were obliged to squeeze themselves up in corners, till Ranulf called out, " Oh, I can't bre-e-eathe !" and Norval had to take him on his knee. When the Sillybilly people came up, the guard ran along the train, calling out, " Plenty of room ! plenty of room ! Every one sit on his own knee, and there's plenty of room ! "

The passengers got very angry at this, and shouted out all sorts of cross replies to the guard.

" There's no need to do that," said one.

" It's not an easy position," said another.

" There's no necessity for it," bawled a fourth.

" It's packing us like negroes," said a fifth.

" It's the *ne plus ultra* of mismanagement," said a sixth.

Those who tried to do it always found that they got on somebody else's knee instead of on their own, which, as it turned out, came to much the same thing, as the moment anybody rose to try to sit down on his own knee, a Sillybillier popped down on his seat.

There was no need for hurry, as the train was only 22 hours and 49 minutes behind time; so, after everybody had with great difficulty got in, and they were packed so tight that the sides of the carriages were bulging out, the station-bell rang for 19 minutes, to show that the train was going to start. Then the guard unscrewed his whistle-nose, wiped it carefully with his pocket-handkerchief, and screwed it on again. It so happened that he fastened it with the wrong end out; and when he blew, he only whistled into himself, so that the driver could not hear; and he had to get the station-master to give him a slap on the back with one of the big tickets, to make the whistling that had stuck in him come out. The train then started, but as there was a bridge just beyond the station, and the carriages were so swelled, it had to be stopped again till the porters had roped the carriages like trunks, to press the sides in and let them pass.

The process made things so tight, that several persons called out, "Oh dear!" At this the porters only laughed, and said, "Dear? it's the cheapest thing you get in twenty-four hours —you get it for nothing."

The train having at last got fairly started, a big fat man, with a jolly broad face, who seemed to get happier and happier the closer the squeeze became, said in a wheezy voice—

"I move that we have a Free-and-Easy."

"Move! that's a good one," said a voice from a corner. "Proposing to move is all very well, but how will you get it done in a squash like this?"

"Well," said the jolly man, "there's nothing like trying."

"No; except trying circumstances, like ours just now."

"We must have a chairman," said the jolly gentleman.

"Here's what you want," said Norval; "I saw him getting in."

E

Everybody looked towards Norval, but in the crowd they could see nothing but a broad, flat, smiling face.

"Why he more than another?" cried several.

"Well, if you could see him, you would know," answered Norval.

Instantly there was a shout — "Clear off, and let us look at him."

Tightly as they were squeezed, they notwithstanding made a tremendous push back from the man beside Norval, till the ropes round the carriage creaked again.

Sure enough, there he was—a chair beyond all doubt, looking as inviting as possible.

"He's just what we want for a Free-and-Easy," said one, "for he's an easy-chair!"

"Come along, be our chair, old boy," said another.

"All right," said he; "but remember, if I agree to act, I won't be sat upon by anybody else; everybody must support the chair."

"All right; we will, we will!" was heard from every side; and those next him whipped him up on their shoulders—from which elevation he grinned a great broad smile.

Everything seemed likely to go right, when a grumpy individual, whom the crush to clear the chair had flattened up against the side of the carriage, till he looked like half of himself, said in slow tones, as if he had only breath for a letter at a time—

"I b-eg-g to mo-o-ve a cou-nt-er mo-shn." Such sighs went from him as he spoke, that it was no wonder he was much reduced in bulk. His words were received with jeers of derision on all sides.

"Counter-motion!" said one; "how can you get a movement out of shop-fixtures?"

" I wa-s a cou-nt-er-jum-per onc-ce, bu-t I a-ad-mit I'm a fi-xt-ure n-ow; bu-t th-at's be-cau-se th-is is a pa-ack-d meet-t-ing."

Nobody felt able to deny that the meeting was packed, so there was a dead silence. The chairman, however, with admirable tact, took up his adversary on his own ground, and said—

· " We don't want any of your pax, so just hold your peace."

" If you don't," said somebody, " we'll turn you out."

" Th-ere w-ill be ro-om to tu-rn the-n; I w-ish yo-u wo-uld do it no-w, fo-r I fe-el tu-rn-ing di-zzy."

" Turning dizzy! really now, you must be a clever party if you can do that," said one.

" You had better withdraw your motion," said the chairman, blandly; " everybody seems against you."

" Ev-er-y-bo-dy-'s pr-ess-ing a-gai-nst me, if th-at's wh-at y-ou mea-n."

" Well, then, we'll admit that you do it under

pressure," said the chairman, cheerily; "we will press you a little more if you wish, but I should think it was a case of *jam satis*."

"*Sic, sic;* I fee-l ve-ry so-so," said the grumpy man; "go-t a s-ing-ing in my ea-rs."

"It's more than we have," said the chairman; "but for you we would have had it long ago— you've kept all the harmony from us; but now for a song. Who'll sing?"

Nobody seemed to like to be first, and there was silence for a minute, when, to the astonishment of everybody, himself included, Ranulf's little voice was heard saying, "I will."

"Bravo, new edition of the Little Songster! sing away!" *

I.

We are three jolly boys, you see,
    Hurrah! hurrah!
We are three jolly boys, you see,
    Hurrah! hurrah!
Norval and Jaques and Ranny—that's me—
As lively as so many crickets are we,

* *Air*—"Johnny come marching home."

And we wish you all a jolly good health, we do !
And we wish you all a jolly good health, we do !

2.

The fairy told us to be good,
　　Hurrah ! hurrah !
The fairy told us to be good,
　　Hurrah ! hurrah !
To be cheery and bright, not sulky or rude—
We nodded our noddles, and said we would ;
And we mean to try, oh, ever so hard, we do !
And we mean to try, oh, ever so hard, we do !

3.

She said we never should tell a lie,
　　Hurrah ! hurrah !
She said we never should tell a lie,
　　Hurrah ! hurrah !
So we'll rather go without pudding or pie,
If it can't be got without telling a lie,
For we mean to hold on tight to truth, we do !
For we mean to hold on tight to truth, we do !

4.

She bid us keep our temper, too,
　　Hurrah ! hurrah !
She bid us keep our temper, too,
　　Hurrah ! hurrah !

So we shall try to put on the screw,
To keep it down whatever we do,
For we mean to be jolly, whatever turns up, we do !
For we mean to be jolly, whatever turns up, we do !

5.

In fact, we'll follow her advice,
Hurrah ! hurrah !
In fact, we'll follow her advice,
Hurrah ! hurrah !
To keep ever free from folly and vice,
And to choose the ways that are noble and nice,
Brave, true gentle men, whatever we say or do !
Brave, true gentle men, whatever we say or do !

6.

Fail we must, but we'll try again,
Hurrah ! hurrah !
Fail we must, but we'll try again,
Hurrah ! hurrah !
For we know, if we work with might and main
And a trusting heart, we'll not strive in vain ;
So we mean to hold on, true to the end, we do !
So we mean to hold on, true to the end, we do !

There was great cheering, and cries, " Bravo,

little un!" when Ranulf finished, and the chairman said—

"The fairy gave you very good advice, so
never forget it. Beware of bad surroundings.
Life's like a railway journey—a great deal de-
pends upon your company not being too fast, and
your having a good carriage, and good coup-
lings. If you maintain a manly upright carriage,
and don't couple yourselves by bad ties, keeping
truth and modesty for your safety-chains, you'll
get on well enough ; but if your life carriage gets
shaky, and your connections loose, and you get
bad buffers about you, you will be apt to come
to grief."

The boys listened attentively as the chairman
spoke, and it is to be hoped that neither they, nor
any other boys who read this, will forget what he
said.

In the meantime, the people seemed not to be
able to get Ranulf's tune out of their heads, and
began to find their own words to carry it on.
From one corner came—

"A spoon of wood is the thing at night,
    Hurrah! hurrah!
A spoon of wood is the thing at night,
    Hurrah! hurrah!
Just swallow it dry, it will clear your sight,
    To see an invisible green so bright!
Oh! we're all jolly tight on our way to Blundertown!
Oh! we're all jolly tight on our way to Blundertown!"

"Stuff and nonsense!" said another, and then he went off himself:—

"Spoon-meat may be good enough for thee,
    Hurrah! hurrah!
Spoon-meat may be good enough for thee,
    Hurrah! hurrah!
But there's nought like a plank of a hare-soup tree,
    Or fresh-roasted ices to make you see
Saw your way through a milestone of brick, you see;
Saw your way through a milestone of brick, you see."

"Shut up!" cried some one from the back of the carriage—"for

"Milestones aren't good looks at all,
    Hurrah! hurrah!
Milestones aren't good looks at all,
    Hurrah! hurrah!

It's easy to see through a stone mile's squall,
    If your eyes are sour and your temper tol-
Erably like a lump of chalk, you see ;
Erably like a lump of chalk, you see."

This seemed to drive a man who had been sitting quiet almost frantic with excitement, and off he went—

" Chalk and stones, and spoons and trees,
            Hurrah ! hurrah !
    Chalk and stones, and spoons and trees,
            Hurrah ! hurrah !
    If your eyes aren't made from a skim-milk cheese,
    What on earth is the good of talking of these ?
For you can't whey what you are talking about, you see ;
For you can't whey what you are talking about, you see."

" Last verse, and moral," said the chairman, with great gravity—

" Such noble thoughts improve the mind,
            Hurrah ! hurrah !
    Such noble thoughts improve the mind,
            Hurrah ! hurrah !
    They belong to the true philosophical kind,
    And the moral is plain to be seen by the blind ;
For it just is this—that a vile un is fiddle-de-dee ;
For it just is this—that a vile un is fiddle-de-dee."

When the noise was at its height, Norval said to the chairman, " It seems to get greater nonsense at every verse."

" To she bure it does," said he ; " you are etting ginto Blunderland, and hings don't thappen there as dey tho in pother laces."

" Yes, indeed," said an old gentleman; " look out at the floor and you will hear with your own toes what cruel of a place this is."

Neither he nor the chairman could help speaking thus, being in Blunderland ; but Norval guessed that the old gentleman meant he was to look and see what kind of a place the train had got into, so turned and gaz-ed out at the win-dow. The first thing he saw  was a man riding with his face to the horse's tail, holding the reins like the tiller-ropes of a boat, which was rather difficult, as he had top-boots on his hands. A little further on came an old man who had a string tied to his leg, the other end of which was held by a pig in a poke-bonnet and a stylish shawl.   Next he saw a very old

man with short trousers and a pinafore, a satchel over his shoulders, and a slate hanging at his side, at whom a boy not older than himself, in a green coat with brass buttons, and a white hat, carrying a gold-headed cane, was looking through an eyeglass.   Jaques had joined Norval, and suddenly called out, "What are they doing in that field?"

"Oh," said the chairman, "they are tigging the durnips."

What they were really doing was emptying carts of large stones on the field.

"Seeding sow for flint-soup," said another.

"Flint-soup would be hard fare, I think," said Jaques; "and besides, how can soup grow?"

"Doesn't it grow cold sometimes?" said the chairman.

Poor Jaques was quite dumbfoundered. He was sure there was some nonsense about it, but he couldn't make it out. However, there was no time for more discussion, as the train began to move very strangely, going along with a series of jumps that shook everybody.

"Treasant plavelling now," said the chairman, smiling sweetly, as the train gave a bump that nearly shook his head off.

"What does it mean?" said Norval.

"Blunderingshire lines are all thade mat way," said the chairman; "it's a strittle lange at first, but it will get used to you."

Bump, bump, bump went the train.

"Oh," said Norval, "I hope there won't be an accident!"

"Accident!" said the old gentleman, "what an

absurd idea to get into anybody's backbone! That would be just the same as common pailways."

" What's a pailway ? " said Ranulf.

" Down the hill, the same as Jack and Jill, I suppose," said Norval.

At this point the train went crash through the end of the station—which was all filled in with glass down to the ground—sending the pieces flying in every direction. Nobody seemed to care the least for this ; and as the boys looked surprised, the chairman said, " We don't go in for class with gare here as they do on French lines. What's the use of glass being so seasily mashed if you don't break it ? "

" It's a gery vood arrangement, because it pets leople know there's a train coming," said one gentleman.

" Yes, and she's an ice arrangement, for she bakes the station warm," said the old gentleman ; " fills him with shivers, you know."

The boys were getting completely puzzled, but there was no time for explanation, as the train stopped almost immediately, and everybody made a rush to get out. You never saw anything so funny as the station was. The big advertisements on the sides were either upside down or had their fronts to the wall. Only a few boards were hung right, and these were as follows :—

ANY OF THE COMPANY'S SERVANTS RECEIVING FEES OR GRATUITIES, WILL HAVE THE AMOUNT DOUBLED

ON APPLYING AT THE

IMPROPER DEPARTMENT.

BY ORDER OF THE MISMANAGER.

IT IS REQUESTED THAT ANY WANT OF ATTENTION

BY THE

COMPANY'S THUMBLERS AND CHAINDROPPERS

BE REPORTED TO

THIS BOARD.

Be fair to Pickpockets.

PORTERS ARE CAUTIONED
NOT
TO SHOW CIVILITY TO PASSENGERS ON ANY
PRETENCE WHATEVER.
INFRINGEMENT OF THIS RULE
WILL BE PRECEDED BY
INSTANT DISMISSAL.

The great clock, instead of using his hands to show the hours, kept putting them to his nose at everybody that looked at him, and the big station-bell stuck out his tongue most impudently. The mess that took place on the platform was extra-ordinary — one point which Blunderland railroads have in common with common ones. The porters were tremendously busy picking their teeth and discussing the affairs of the nation, and smiled blandly to those who asked them to do anything. When at last they did move, their proceedings were of the strangest. One took hold of a lady and dragged her along the platform, singing out, "Whose baggage is this?" Another seized two fashionable young ladies, put them on his truck, and accosting an old dowager, asked, "Are these your traps, mum?" A third pick-ed up two children by the legs, swung them over his shoul-

der, and asked their father, "Shall I put the small things inside the cab, sir?" The boys, seeing what a mess things were in, ran off to get out of the station as fast as they could, for they heard the station-master say that he thought they were

F

lost luggage, and had better be locked up.   They
made first for a large placard
marked "THE WAY OUT," with a

hand pointing on it, but found that it led into a
stone wall.

"Everything seems to go by contrary here,"
said Norval; "let us take the direction that seems
least likely."   So seeing a placard marked "No
passage this way," they went straight down the
archway opposite it, and found themselves out-

side the station at once, and in a broad roadway. The foot-pavement was in the middle of the street, and the road on either side of it next the houses, which would have been very inconvenient had it not been that, as in Blundertown things are quite different from other towns, the roadway was beautifully clean. On the opposite side of the street from the station there was a building which, from its grand proportions and ornamental style, the boys thought must be a palace. As they stood looking at it, a black board, such as they had often seen used at school for writing sums on, made its appearance at the door and gravely walked down the steps. The board had two arms, one hand grasping a pointer, and the other a piece of chalk and a towel. It came forward, walking very clumsily with its wooden feet, and the whole appearance was so ridiculous that the boys could not help laughing. The board seemed to see this somehow, raised his piece of chalk and wrote on himself,

" *Do you know who I am ?* "

The boys confessed they did not. The board raised the hand with the towel and wiped himself, and then wrote,

" I am the School Board,"

pointing to the words with a grand sweep of the stick, as much as to say, "What do you think

of that?" They were not at all overawed by
this great announcement, and the ridiculous
flourish of the pointer made them look at one
another and laugh again. At this the board
looked blacker than ever, and angrily wiping
himself wrote,

" *You must make a bow to the board.*"

" Oh, all right!" said Jaques; and they all made
a low mock bow, shaking with laughter. When
they raised their heads after bowing, they saw that
the board was wiped again, and that it wrote,

" *If you do that you will break me.*"

" How can laughing break you?" said Norval.

" *Solvuntur risu tabulæ.*

Boards are broken with laughter.—

Free translation."

wrote the board.

" Well, then, we won't any more," said Norval;
and they all kept down their laughter as well as
they could.

"That is kind," wrote the board. "We too often have splits in our School Boards; but as you have stopped, I feel sound again."

"Feel sound! surely you can't do that; hear it, you mean," said Jaques.

Board.—"You mean what? Finish your sentence. Boards are generally thought extravagant, and not mean."

Jaques.—"I don't mean you're mean. I mean you mean——"

Board.—"If you are doing a verb, it is—

I mean.		I mean.
Thou meanest.	*not*	You mean."

Jaques.—"But I did not intend to say that you were mean or meanest; indeed I didn't."

Board.—"You said mean, didn't you?"

Jaques.—"Yes."

Board.—"And you did mean to say mean."

Jaques.—"Yes; but——"

Board.—"Stop. You did mean mean when you said mean."

Jaques.—"Yes, but I didn't mean——"

Board.—" Stop. If you did mean mean, how can you say that you didn't mean ? "

Jaques.—" But when I say mean, I don't mean the mean that you mean. You mean mean something ; it's unfair."

Board.—" Not by any manner of means. You need not put on an indignant mien in addition to all the other means."

Jaques.—" But I mean to say that I did not mean to say the mean that you mean, when you say mean, but did mean the mean that isn't mean."

Board.—" Take care, young man ; you will become a hopeless prodigal if you don't look better after your means."

How long this kind of thing might have gone on it is impossible to tell ; but it was put an end to by a little boy coming out of the school, and taking the School Board by the ear, saying—

" What are you idling your time here for, sir ? be off into school at once."

" Oh dear, sir ! please, sir," whined the board,

as he piped, or rather pipeclayed, his eye, " I
won't do it any more, sir. Let me off this time,
sir; ah, you might, sir !"

The boy let the board go, and it immediately
walked its chalks into school, wiping its eyes with
the towel. He then turned to our heroes, and
said politely—

" These School Boards are a perfect nuisance,
what with the power of rating they have got, and
the power of prating they assume, things are
coming to a pretty pass."

In this our heroes thoroughly agreed with him.

" Perhaps you would like to step in and see our
mode of tuition."

They were quite proud at the idea of being
treated as visitors, like the grown-up ladies and
gentlemen who came to their own school, and
said they would like it very much, so the boy
led the way to the building.

Norval, thinking that a visitor should ask questions, said—

" What branches do you teach ?"

"Oh, all kinds," answered the boy. "Growing branches, green branches, lopped branches, rotten branches, branches of the service, railway branches, railway switches, courteous boughs, sprigs of nobility, and many others. Do you twig?"

"But what things do you teach?"

"We don't teach them at all. Putting pupils up to a thing or two is not approved of."

"But I mean what is your division of subjects?"

"We don't cut up subjects here; we have no anatomical class."

"But," said Norval, who had seen an education report in a newspaper, "do you follow any standard in your teaching?"

"No, there's no flagging with us. We try to keep in advance in our training; we go in for the truck system, so as to keep in the van."

They were now entering one of the class-rooms, so that Norval's questioning was brought to a close, leaving him quite as wise as he was before, for which it is to be hoped he was sufficiently grateful.

The grammar lesson was going on, and in the course of a few minutes they had illustrations of various moods—dull moods, sulky moods, cheerful moods, rude moods, and good moods. They also learned a new point in grammar—that there are an indefinite number of cases. Norval objected when this was stated; but the teacher, who had a dominiering look, though an M A ciated Fellow, met his objection at once.

"Beg pardon, sir; we do not in our modern school submit to the teaching of old-fashioned grammars. We stick to facts, sir — to facts. Thomas, prove to the gentleman that there are more cases than are stated in the old grammars."

Thomas, who went by the nickname of Soft Tommy—being bred though not born a duffer— tried to look crusty, and did not rise.

"Case No. 1, a case of obstinacy," said the teacher, with a grand air. "Then there are sad cases, strong cases, long cases, card-cases, cases of conscience, cases of instruments, cases of divorce, dressing-cases, hard cases, puzzling cases, pencil-cases, cases of brandy, cases of collision, packing-cases, caucases, ukases, ca-sas——"

How long he might have gone on nobody can tell; but the small boy that acted as conductor, seizing a cane, began be-labouring the teacher with it most vigorously. The master seemed to take this quite as a matter of course (as indeed the class did also), and calmly brought his speech to a close, say-ing, in a voice broken by  sobs, "and lastly, for the present, a case of dis-cipline."

The smallest boy in the class now walked boldly forward, and said—

"We've had plenty of your cases, and, in our present mood, decline going on with this intense sort of nonsense. Give us some history; come on, old boy!" Saying this, he gave him a poke in the ribs.

Our heroes could hardly help feeling a considerably uncomfortable sensation at the thought of what would have happened behind them had they behaved to their teacher at home as the class were doing; but instead of this one acting as they would have expected, he turned and said—

" I beg your pardon, young gentlemen, if I have detained you too long at grammar."

" Well, well, take care it does not happen again," ran in a murmur through the class, as the boys produced their history books.

" Now then, old stick in the mud !" said the top boy to the teacher, "read us that jolly bit about the battle, and don't make any mistakes, or you'll catch it." As he said this, he and all the other boys pulled out their handkerchiefs, and made them up with knots.

The reading began ; and the teacher, probably from fear, made every now and then some trifling blunder. Whenever this occurred, the whole class rushed on him and belaboured him with the knotted handkerchiefs. Our heroes were at first afraid he would be seriously hurt; but as, being a Board teacher, he paid no more attention to the blows than if he had been made of wood, they soon began rather to enjoy the scene. The history lesson was as follows :—

" Hannibal, at the head of the invincible Roman legions, which had just got their rout,* marched on Poke Stogis. His infantry was augmented by an Amazon corps from the new British Woman's Rights League, the special feature of which was, that it allowed talking in the ranks, and, indeed, used gossip and scandal as potent means of defeating its foes. The cavalry, who were greatly improved in musketry since one General Shoot had got the command, were mounted on highly-mettled steeds, cast by the

---

* It is perhaps not generally known that before troops march forth to victory, they are first routed by the Quartermaster-General's Department. Should the reader think this a joke, he will probably say it is a very poor one; but if he will take the trouble to ask any of his military friends, he will find that they think it anything but a joke that they get routed so often.—ED.

Board of Ordnance, and splendidly broken, espe-
cially about the knees. On nearing Poke Stogis,
Hannibal was met by General Wattyler, who
commanded the king's troops. Hannibal, true to
the traditions of the house of Hapsburg, rode in
a Magna Carta—a war-chariot invented by King
John when his subjects were taking liberties—
while the General bestrode a 50-inch bycycle that
had been presented to him by Ptolemy on the
occasion of the opening of the Fiji water-works,
at which the General, who was a freemason, had,
in Scotch parlance, proved himself a very wat
tyler indeed. The inhabitants of Poke Stogis,
as is usual in tropical countries, regaled the
troops on both sides with gooseberry-fool, after
which the battle commenced in a field, and in
earnest. After two hours' hard fighting, during
which splendid reinforcements arrived in Hansom
cabs from Connecticut and Pondicherry, and
after tossing up a halfpenny to decide which
army they should join, went half to one side and
half to the other, an adjournment took place for

luncheon, and another repast of sponge-cakes and ginger-beer was provided by the energy of the Major and Common Council of Poke Stogis, who, with that true nobility which is the best evidence of genuine rank, drew the corks with their own hands. These additional draughts added greatly to the strength of both sides, and comforted the combatants much, as they knew that those of them who might fall in the battle had their bier already provided for them. Before resuming hostilities, each commander addressed his troops in a few soul-stirring  words. But small fragments of these celebrated speeches have been handed down to the present day; yet these are so valuable, that it is thought well here to reproduce them. Their noble sentiment and stirring patriotism may well cause them to be engraven upon the hearts of the rising generation. Lest any words unworthy of the rest should be inserted, it is thought preferable to leave blanks where the actual expressions are not known. Hannibal said—

. . . . . on this occasion, it is with . . .

. . . . indeed, I may say . . . . . ten thousand . . . . . . indeed, less and less

. . . . . . may I not say . . . words would fail me . . . . brave soldiers of the

. . . . enemy . . . . . . victory is

. . . . nay was . . . . . perhaps may be . . . . . . disgrace . . . . shall add no more . . . .

"If these disjointed fragments convey so much, well might it be asked, What may not the rest have been? The reader must answer this for himself. Of General Wattyler's speech still less has been preserved. In fact, but for forty-nine h's, which the pious affection of the citizens of Poke Stogis collected, and preserved in carbolic acid, history would be a blank regarding it. All honour to the men who spared no labour to preserve to a grateful posterity these valuable records of a warrior and a hero. When the memory of thousands of greater places is lost in futurity, the glory Poke Stogis has haitchieved in handing down to us the droppings of a great warrior's lips will be blazoned on the scroll of fame.

" The battle having recommenced, was so hotly contested that the thermometer rose to 549 degrees of Fahrenheit, and 272 men on one side

perished, drowned in the surging tide of battle ; while 74 of the opposing troops were roasted (although it was Friday) before the slow fire of the enemy. Both sides won a decisive victory, and captured the whole of the enemy's artillery. A noble pillar, 1 foot 7½ inches high, still marks the spot on which Hannibal and Wattyler ad-

G

justed the terms of the general order to the troops, thanking them in the name of King Cole (not the old one, but Parrot Cole, surnamed the Chatterer) for the glorious stampede by which they had turned the fortunes of the day. The event was celebrated in Poke Stogis by a grand illumination, in which seven bunches of dips, four boxes of Bryant & May's matches, and two rows of fusees were expended—an extravagance not often perpetrated by a corporation so careful of the public money as that of Poke Stogis. The people shouted till they were hoarse, —they belonging to the class that cheers though not inebriates."

This concluded the history lesson, and the school was then exercised in prose composition. Want of space forbids the production of more than a single specimen of the papers written ; but the following is a fair one :—

THEME.—*Cloe's parents desire to wed her to Strephon, the eldest son of a noble house, and bid her accept his suit. She, being in love with Alexis,*

*the younger son, secretly meets him. They are dis-
covered. Cloe is rebuked for her heartlessness,
and Alexis languishes in a prison.—Moral.*

" In such a state from heat so great, Alexis
groaned and Cloe moaned, as through the wood,
in loving mood, they made their way, till close
of day; when homeward turning with cheeks just

burning, to 'scape a shower they sought a bower,
in which they rested and playful jested, and did
discuss, promiscuous, their hopes and fears for
future years, till moon uprose and did disclose,

'neath graceful skirt, drawn up from dirt, her ankle neat near two great feet, to anxious Pa, who cried, ' Ha, ha ! I've found you out ; ' then with a shout, flew on her swain and called his train, who held the stripling in their grip, and made him sleep in dungeon deep ; while pretty Cloe wept in woe, as angry mater did soundly rate her, rustling with fuss, calling her, ' hussey, brazen jade, wer't not afraid ? how couldst thou do't ? Lean to the suit of younger son, devoid of money ! Secret wooings ! Hein ! pretty doings ! ' "

" MORAL.—This may suffice as good advice, to lovers to keep skirts from view, and draw their toes well in *sub rosa,* when in

bower at evening hour, and making spoons by light of moons."

When the prose composition was over, the teacher was about to commence another lesson, but the small boy who had been so active with the cane before, coolly walked up to the desk, took the teacher's watch out of his pocket, and holding it up called out—

" Mischief-class hour !"

In a moment the air was full of shouts and yells, slates and books, satchells and ink-bottles. Norval and his brothers were quite picklish enough to feel tempted to enjoy the fun ; but seeing that the mischief was going far beyond what ought to be joined in, he seized Jaques and Ranulf, and made for the door. Fortunately for the boys, the teacher was between them and the class on their way out ; and two ink-bottles, five pieces of india-rubber, a blotting-blad, and a handful of slate pencil, that came flying in their direction, were stopped by the body of the master, who; being a Board teacher, was not, as the boys expected,

floored by the missiles, but beamed pleasantly
as if all was oakay, and the sensation so deali-
cious, that he wood like some more treemen-
dously.   Just as the boys were getting out at the
door, the whole class rushed upon the teacher,
and made him fast to the wall with his own
nails, where he stuck with a plank look on his
plane face, as if he was now bored through and
through. Somehow the whole thing seemed to
everybody engaged to be so ordinary an occur-
rence that the three boys felt no alarm, as they
would have done under other circumstances ; and
as they got out and shut the door, had a hearty
laugh at the ludicrous scene they had witnessed.

On reaching the street they began to stroll
through the town, amusing themselves by looking in at the shop-windows.   There was plenty
of food for merriment, as things were mixed up
in a very curious way.   The contents of one
window were, a leg of mutton, the Children's
Friend, a bottle of senna, six farthing dips, two
bunches of radishes, an oyster, a wooden leg,.

and a stuffed goose. In another, over which was painted upside down " Rafé and Cestaurant," there were a millstone, a wooden shoe, three india-rubber goloshes, a can of train-oil, two white hats, a brass knocker, and a dead cat. A shop marked " Plug-gist, licensed by the Packulty," exhibited a drum, two sucking pigs, a magic-lantern, five cocked-hats, a green cotton umbrella, two packs of cards, a tin soldier, and a frying-pan. The notices in the windows were also very queer. One said, " No credit given, except without security. Any person paying ready money will be handed over to the police." Close beside this was another : " Price down from 5s. to 7s. 9d. each." The boys thought either sum would have been rather dear, as the ticket was upon a common peg-top, such as they had often bought for twopence. Another label bore, "Try our Totalfailure Mixture, strongly remmocended by the Boil College of Imposicians." It would take too long to speak of all the funny things they saw; besides, it is always bad taste to talk too much " shop." If any one would like to hear more on that subject, he has only to address a polite note to

MESSRS NORVAL, JAQUES, RANULF, & COMPANY,

The Nurseryfun Works,

Skrumpshustown,

enclosing five thousand stamps, when he will receive by return of post a copy of the most amusing shop-label they saw in Blundertown. If he considers the price too high, let him remember the poet's query—

"What is aught but as 'tis valued?"

and if he thinks the answer is Naught, he can judge himself what is the difference, if N y.

Affairs in the street were quite as queer as in the shops. While the boys were looking in at a window, a silvery voice behind them called out, "Stalest Tellacrams—Last week's paper at double price;" and turning round they saw a young lady, dressed in perfect taste, the only blunders about her being that she had no hair on her head but her own, which was neither dyed nor bleached, nor combed down over her eyes *à la* pet terrier, and that she walked like a human being, not as ladies in the ordinary world do, with their heels perched up on things like a couple of inches cut

off the legs of a chair, and wearing their dresses so tight, that their knees seem to be tied together with tape.   A footman followed her, who had the calves of his legs in front, and the tie of his cravat at the back, and whose neck was not at all stiff, but shook like a shape of calves-foot jelly.

He carried a quantity of newspapers, wrapped in scented envelopes. Instead of getting pennies for her newspapers, the young lady, whenever anybody took one, curtsied low, and kissing her hand, gravely gave them a penny, saying, " Thanks, thanks—a thousand, thousand thanks; Telegraphina will never forget your kindness."

The people, when they met in the street, instead of passing, walked straight up to each other, bumped one another heavily, and then went on smiling as if all was right. While Norval was gazing after the pretty young lady with the newspapers, an old dame, with a reticule on her head and a bonnet full of apples in her hand, made straight at him. Norval got out of the way, and she nearly fell on her nose, the apples rolling out on the pavement.

"What a rude old man, to be sure!" said she, scowling at Norval.

" I only got out of the way, ma'am, if you mean me by old man," said he.

" And what's the use of people who are not in

the way when they are wanted ? " said she. " Old men like you——"

" I'm not an old man," said Norval, interrupting.

" When were you born ? " said the old lady, snappishly.

" Eight years ago," said Norval.

" Then you're eight years old." Norval did not see any answer to this, and she went on, " Does your papa ever tell lies ? "

" No," said Norval, indignantly.

" Doesn't he call you his little man sometimes ? "

" Yes."

" Then you're old and you're a man, so you're an old man."

Norval did not quite see it—" I don't feel old," he said.

" How can I know how you feel," replied the old lady, " when you won't bump me ? Oh ! " she added, screwing up her lips and clasping her hands, " I do love a bumper ! Is your name Tom ? "

" No," said Norval.

" That's a pity; there's no bumper like an old
Tom ; he's a noble spirit, always ginoowine."

" I can't follow you," said Norval.

" And did I say I wanted you to follow me ?
Gals have no followers here ; I only wanted my
regular bump."

Norval having a grandfather who was fond of
phrenology, had picked up a smattering, and was
just going to say that he thought it was only silly
people that wanted regular bumps, when suddenly
the old lady called out, "Where are my pears ?
there were four of them."

Jaques and Ranulf, who had picked up the
apples, had been standing ready to hand them
back to her ever so long.

" I beg your pardon," said Jaques, "they are
apples."

" I say they're pears," said the old lady, testily.
" How many have you ?"

" Eight," said Jaques.

" Well, and isn't that four pairs ? I always
like to buy them pared ; it saves knives and

trouble," said she. "It's a pity that a boy like you should be a beggar."

"I'm not a beggar," said Jaques.

"Didn't you beg my pardon?"

"Yes."

"Those who beg are beggars, that's sure," said she.

Just at this moment a policeman came up. He took off his helmet, and making a low bow, said, "I heard the word beg. May I take the great liberty of inquiring whether any one has thought proper to beg? and if so, from whom, and for what? If for anything real, good and well; but if merely from politeness or courtesy, then to be visited with the utmost severity of the law."

Jaques, who had always been taught fearlessly to speak the truth, said at once, "I begged the old lady's pardon," half doubting what would happen. To his great surprise the policeman turned round sharp on the old lady, and asked, "Did this boy beg your pardon?"

"Yes," said she.

"Then, madam, with peelings of the deepest

fain, it is my duty to inform you that you must at once be led to the court."

"The court!" screamed the old lady; "it has been my ambition for fifty years to be courted, and now it has come at last."

"It has, madam; you are now about to be presented at court by the aid of the police. Will your Majesty deign to proceed?"

"Majesty!" said she; "I can't understand it."

"Let me endeavour to make it plain," said the constable, with a wave of his hand like a professor lecturing. "Will your gracious Majesty deign to inform me whether I am correct in saying that this boy begged your pardon?"

"Yes."

"And would your Highness further permit me to inquire whether it is or is not a fact that begging is contrary to law?"

"Yes."

"May I also be suffered humbly and respectfully to put the question, whether anybody can pardon people for breaking the law, except the Queen?"

" No."

" Then I reverentially request permission of your gracious Majesty to point out that as you were asked to pardon when he broke the law, you must be the queen."

" But I've got no crown," said she, quite puzzled.

" I must be condescendingly excused for venturing to differ from your Serene Highness. If you will feel for it, you will find you have a crown to your head."

" Why, so I have," said she, and suddenly drawing herself up, and assuming an air of most ridiculous dignity, added, " What, ho! bring hither my sceptre."

The boys could scarcely keep in their laughter, and the difficulty increased when the policeman produced his baton, and going down on one knee handed it to the old lady, who immediately aimed a fierce blow at his head, crying,—

" Down with every one that has a crown except myself!"

The policeman mildly replied, " Your Majesty,

I haven't got a crown in the world; my missus doesn't allow me more than 4 and 9 a-week for pocket-money."

"Just as well for you; those who are limited to four and ninepence can feel proper respect for a sovereign," said the old lady; " now for our court." So saying, she began to perform a most wild *minuet de la cour*, the policeman beating time with his hands. Then order-

ing him to take off his greatcoat, she fastened it on as a train, and set off for the court.

The policeman went first, playing a grand march on a Jew's harp, which he produced from his pocket. It was as big as a fire-shovel, but this did not matter, as he had a mouth reaching from ear to ear. The old lady followed, holding her baton-sceptre up, and with her long, sharp chin cocked so high in the air that you could have hung a hat upon it. The policeman's music made her quite lively, and she began to sing, with a chorus to each verse, which ran thus,—

Hey tiddy - iddy - tiddy, Hey tiddy - iddy - tiddy,

Hey   tiddy - iddy - tiddy, tum - tum - tum.

during the singing of which she skipped about from one side to the other in a most lively manner.

> I never thought to see
> The day I queen should be ;
> It's come at last, however,
> You well may cry—"I never !"
>   Hey tiddy iddy tiddy, &c., &c.
>
> Nor I, but still it's poz,
> However strange, because

Policeman says 'tis so ;
X is 'xact, you know.
    Hey tiddy iddy tiddy, &c., &c.

Our reign shall last so long,
You'll need umbrellas strong ;
Woe to the minion's skin
Who sports a gingham thin !
    Hey tiddy iddy tiddy, &c., &c.

A sovereign we shall be,
Ruling land and sea
In straighter lines than youc
Ould find in copy-book.
    Hey tiddy iddy tiddy, &c., &c.

We'll have a Parliament
Cake and wine event
Every day or two,
Invites select and few.
    Hey tiddy iddy tiddy, &c., &c.

To have a feast of rea
Son at our royal tea ;
Likewise a flow of soul,
By Punch from royal bowl.
    Hey tiddy iddy tiddy, &c., &c.

And nominate a Prime
Minister of rhyme ;

Pros and Cons shall banished be,
Except conundrums after tea.
    Hey tiddy iddy tiddy, &c., &c.

Look out for famous sport,
For we are going to court;
So bachelors beware,
And let no caitiff dare
    Hey tiddy iddy tiddy, &c., &c.

Refuse our royal suit
Of livery, and put
On his own airs instead,
Or off shall go his head.
    Hey tiddy iddy tiddy, &c., &c.

Each time the old lady took up the chorus, she skipped about from one side to the other with a briskness that did her credit; and as she marched and tripped along the street, the policemen she passed joined the procession, each producing an instrument from his pocket, so that soon the old lady had a band before her, playing most vigorously on the following :—

    A Jew's Harp.
    A Penny Trumpet.

Three Threepenny Fid-
dles.
A Handbell.
Two Twopenny Flutes.
A Mouth Accordion.
A Triangle.
A Pair of Bones;

and the inspector led
the band, with his hat
fastened to his waist-
belt, keeping them to
their beat by drumming
in a spirited manner on
the crown of it with a
pair of batons.

The boys tried very
hard to find out what the
tune of the verses was,
but could make nothing
of it. All the melody
seemed to rest in the

chorus instead of running through the song. The
people in the streets, however, were evidently
greatly delighted with it, as, the moment the
procession came within hearing, they all stood
still and began gravely to beat time with their
sticks and umbrellas, those who had none wagging
their heads up and down, like China mandarins.
The boys laughed heartily when they saw several
dozen umbrellas, sticks, and heads solemnly waving about, while the policemen squeaked and
croaked, banged and tinkled, on their instruments,
and the people slowly turned round their backs
and bowed low to the houses as the old lady
passed. Whenever she, in skipping about, came
near any of the people who were bowing, she took
a rise out of them by administering a sound whack
with the baton-sceptre, which knocked them down,
shouting, " Rise, Sir What's-your-name Thing-
ammy," which the poor fellows did with a very
beknighted look. Presently they arrived at a
large building, at the door of which the policemen turned aside to let the old lady enter, and

having played a final flourish, repocketed their instruments. The old lady on reaching the door turned round, and finding the policeman who had given her the baton waiting, she grasped it firmly, saying—

"I'll give it to you," and, suiting the action to

the utterance, she brought it down bang as hard as she could, as he bowed low, so that he fell flat on the pavement.

"Rise, Sir Charle——"

"Stop, stop!" he cried; "don't turn a day constable into a knight."

" Back to your beat," said she, majestically.

" I think it's rather beat to my back," replied
he, although, curiously enough, he did not appear at all discomposed or hurt.

" Take yourself up."

" We take others up, not ourselves; besides,
you've battened me down."

" Oh, you downy fellow!"

" Yes, you can't get a rise out of me, that's plain."

" X plain yourself," said she.

" No pretty Bobby-she should say," said he.

" Move on!" cried she—" move on, siree!"

" Peeler of the State, I stands," said he.

Suddenly some one rushed out at the door
(knocking the old lady so that she tumbled over
the policeman), and coming up to the boys said,
" Are you judges of sweet things?"

" I should rather think so," replied Jaques.

" Then come along at once," said he; and before they had time to think, he hurried them up-
stairs into a room where three pompous-looking
attendants in white coats and enormous black

neckcloths dressed them up in grand robes, put
immense full-bottomed wigs on their heads, and
opening a door, pointed to three large chairs.
The boys went in and sat down on the chairs,
while everybody in the court rose up, making a
low bow, and a crier called out—

"All persons, without any further ado before
my Lords the Justices of Assize so small Boyer
and Determiner, and Jug ale Delivery, draw beer
and give to attendants."

This announcement about beer might have appeared to be an aberration on the crier's part, had
it not been that, as is usual in criminal courts,
there were plenty of queer mugs among the people
in the building.

The boys hardly knew what to think of their
new position. Norval and Jaques were rather
overawed by their robes. Ranulf had got between
his brothers, and so was seated in the Lord Chief
Justice's chair. At first he looked as grave as a
judge, which was just what he ought to have done
in the circumstances; but after a little he glanced

round at Norval, and seeing him in his wig, which came down to his waist, was just on the point of bursting out laughing, when the Clerk of Court, who wore green goggles as large as macaroons, peered over the Bench

from below, saying, " If yer Ludship pleases," and
sat down again.

"I hope I do please," said Ranulf. " Papa always bids us try to please."

" Your Lordship pleases me very much," said a
charming voice from the prisoner's dock, in which
stood a lovely lady, dressed in full Court costume,
feathers and all, who kissed her daintily-gloved
hand to Ranulf.

" But I thought we were brought here as judges
of sweet things," said Jaques.

The Clerk of Court peering over the bench
again, said, "'Xac'ly so, m' Lud ; the sweetest
thing in prisoners we've had for a long time,
m' Lud," and sat down again.

" What is she charged with ? " said Norval.

" P'tty lasseny, m' Lud."

" Pretty lasseny ! " said Jaques aside to Norval.
" I am sure she is guilty of that."

" But," said Norval, " what is she charged with
doing ? "

" Stealing a heart, m' Lud."

Norval, who had once been in court at a trial,

thought the right thing to do was to take a note; so, seizing an enormous pen that was on the bench, he wrote, repeating aloud as he went on, " Prisoner charged with stealing a tart."

" The person who stole tarts was a knave, and I thought a knave was a man ? " said Ranulf.

" Yes," said Norval ; " but you know the women want to do what the men do nowadays."

" I've heard of their wanting rights," said Jaques; " but stealing isn't a right, it's a wrong, isn't it ? "

" Never mind," said Norval; " it won't do to appear not to understand. Ranny, you're the old judge, you know, because you're in the middle, so you must ask the questions. You had better ask what the prisoner's name is. Now, look grave," said he, as he observed the dimples in his brother's cheeks beginning to show again.

Ranulf pursed his lips up very tight, and then said, " I want to know what the pretty lady's name is ? "

" No, no," said Norval; " prisoner."

" I want to know the pretty prisoner's name ? " said Ranulf.

" No, no—just prisoner," said Norval; "say it again."

" Well, then, I want to know the just prisoner's name?" said Ranulf.

" Just so, m' Lud," said the Clerk, bobbing up; "prisoner's name is Victoria Lawsenj. Yer Ludship had better ask her to plead."

Norval whispered to Ranulf, " Tell her she's charged with stealing a tart. Ask whether she is guilty or not guilty."

Ranulf looked as grave as he could, and said " Victoria Lawsenj, you are charged with stealing a tart——"

" Beg pardon, m' Lud," said the Clerk, starting up; "some m'stake, my Lud——"

Ranulf began again, " Victoria Lawsenj, you are charged with stealing a tart and some steak."

" Must pray yer Ludsh'p t' excuse me 'gain;" "yer Ludship said tart and steak."

" Was that the wrong order?" said Ranulf, meekly; " then I'll say steak and tart."

" But, m' Lud, the steak is a mistake, and the tart is another."

" Very well," said Ranulf; " I'll say that she is charged with stealing a female steak—cow-beef— and that the tart was not really a tart but a beef-steak pie."

" But, m' Lud," said the Clerk; "really, m' Lud, yer Ludship knows best, m' Lud, of course; but, m' Lud, I would suggest that your Ludship said tart instead of heart."

Here Norval, remembering what he had seen in court, broke in, " But tart is right; it must be right—I've got it in my notes."

This completely flabbergasted the Clerk, who gasped a feeble " M' Lud," and sank down in his seat in despair.

Jaques, practical as usual, whispered to Ranulf, "Never mind whether it's a tart or a heart; just say, ' You are charged with stealing a tart, or a heart, or something. Are you guilty or not guilty ?' "

Ranulf took this advice; and turning to the lady, who was gracefully fanning herself, he asked her the question, only he got confused towards the end, and made it—" Are you gilded or not gilded ? "

" Oh, my Lord," said the lady, " there's no gilt about me ; I'm as true as steel."

Up started the Clerk.

" Take down, m' Lud, that she says it's true she stole."

" No, I didn't ; I only steeled," said she.

" Steeeled ! " said the Clerk, contemptuously ; " how do you spell ' steeeeled ' ? "

" S-t-e-e-l-e-d, you old goose ! "

" Yer Ludship sees how bad she is ; her manner's bad, her grammar's bad, and her spelling's bad. Your Ludship had better add another count for murder."

" Murder of what ? " said Jaques.

" The Queen's English, m' Lud."

" That would be a great many murders, for there are more than thirty million English," said Jaques, who had learned the population in his geography book ; " how could she murder so many?"

The Clerk was quite puzzled at this, and tried

to look as wise as he could, which was not very wise, but otherwise. There was a long pause, during which the prisoner ate an ice and drank a cool beverage that were brought to her by a powdered footman, after which she looked brighter and lovelier than ever, while everybody else in court was miserable with stuffiness and heat.

"Could not we have ices too?" said Ranulf, eyeing the tray eagerly.

The footman said nothing, but turning round made a low bow, walked up to the bench, and as the boys held out their hands for ices, gravely shook his head, made another low bow, and walked out.

By this time the Clerk had recovered himself, and a jury having been called, they were got into the jury-box. This was a matter of some difficulty, as the box was made without any door, and the jurymen were seized by ushers and thrown over the partition, tumbling in a confused heap. When the whole twelve had been thrown over, they presented a sorry spectacle of torn clothes

and dusty faces.   There were no seats in the box,
but the ushers threw in some chairs on the top
of the jurymen, who appeared to take all as

a matter of course.
The plaintiff was then
called forward, and a
large wooden box
placed over him by
the ushers, who pad-
locked it down and
then sat on the top
of it.

" Why do you lock him up ? " said Jaques.

"Shall 'ave to beg yer Ludship's pardon,' said the Clerk; "we don't lock him up, we lock him down."

"But why do you put him under a case?" said Jaques.

"To prevent him getting up case, m' Lud."

Jaques himself seemed rather shut up at this, and Norval, moved again by what he had once seen at a trial, said, "What is your name?"

"John," said the voice, out of the box.

"It should be Jack, when he's in a box, shouldn't it?" said Ranulf; "and he ought to start up, oughtn't he?"

"Oh, he will be sure to do that," said the lady; "he always was an upstart, indeed he was, my dear—Lord, I mean," said she, correcting herself with a smile.

"John What?" Norval went on.

"No, my name's not John What," said the voice from the box; "it's John Doe."

"That's strange," said Jaques; "I thought the case was about a heart, not about a doe."

I

"Yes, my Lud, but the charge is that she stole a Doe's heart," said the Clerk.

"Doe and hart, hart and doe; I don't think I'll ever understand it," said Ranulf, with a sigh.

"P'raps if yer Ludship would keep in mind that in Doe *versus* Roe——"

"Oh dear, oh dear! here's a roe now; that's another staggerer," cried Jaques.

"Never mind," whispered Norval—"look solemn, and make believe you know all about it."

The examination of John Doe then began.

"How long have you known the prisoner?"

"Various lengths. I have known her from 2 feet 3 inches long to 5 feet 7½ inches long, as she is now. But even now she is sometimes pretty short with me. I've known her so long, in short, that the longer I knew her the more I got to long after her."

"Well, I don't want to know anything about long after; I mean, when did you first come across her?"

"I cross her! I never crossed her in my life.

She had her own way as long as I knew her; it was she that was cross with me."

" But I want to know the length of your acquaintance ? "

" Some of my acquaintances are long and some short."

" How shall I put it ? Tell me, once for all, when you first met her."

" When I first met her ? I met her when I least expected it."

" Really this is intolerable. I want you to tell me what was the time at which your first meeting took place."

" Wild thyme, I think; but I'm no botanist, you know."

" Tut, tut ! At what period of time was it ? "

" It wasn't a period of thyme, it was a bank of thyme."

" Will you answer, sir ? Give me the date of your first meeting."

" We had no dates at our first meeting, only

raisins; and we ate them all, so I cannot give you
any."

"A fig for your dates and raisins!   I wish I

could get at the *raison d'être* of your answers.
How can I put the question?"

"That's just what I want to know.   How can
you put such stupid questions?"

"M' Lud, what am I to do? I can make nothing of this witness."

Norval, who had learned a little Latin, replied, "Do you mean that you can annihilate him?"

"No, m' Lud, but I can't make head or tail of him."

"Never mind his head, and let him manage his own tail. Perhaps he's a bit of a wag."

"Very well, m' Lud. Now, then, tell your story."

"I'm not a story-teller. I always tell the truth."

"Yes, yes, but come on with your own tale."

"Tail! I haven't a tail. I'm not one of your Darwin monkey-people."

The lady in the dock gave such a merry laugh at this, that she infected the whole court. Ranulf went into such fits, that his wig slipped down to his chin, and an usher had to come up to the bench and slap him on the back to bring him round. Norval recovered first, and putting on as grave a face as he could, said to Jaques and Ranulf, "Don't be silly; judges are always stern

and grumpy, so we must be too; and turning to
John Doe, said, "What is your complaint against
her? Did she steal your heart?"

"No, my Lord; it was her own heart."

"Her own heart! How can that be? How
could her own heart be stolen by her?"

"I never said it was stolen, my Lord, I only said
she steeled it."

"Surely that's bad grammar, again," whispered
Jaques.

"But I want to know," said Norval, "how could
she steal what was her own?"

"Well, my Lord, you see I gave her my whole
heart."

"Gave it her? I thought you charged her
with stealing it?"

"No, my Lord, never! It was her own she
steeled."

"Well, well," said Norval, "go on; try to ex-
plain it in your own way."

"This was the way, my Lord; I wanted her to
be my sweetheart."

" That's right, my Lord," said the lady; "and I was tart without the sweet, I admit."

" Yes, my Lord, a regular Tartar; when I gave her my whole heart, she steeled hers against me."

" True," said the prisoner; "your Lordship must know he came with so much brass, that I could only meet him with irony, particularly as I fancied he was after the tin."

Practical Jaques here broke in once more, saying, "Would it not put the matter all right if she gave you back your heart?"

" Oh, but, my Lord, I gave her my whole heart, and she's broken it."

" That need not be a difficulty," said the lady; " I'll soon put it together; I'm very good at a patchwork quilt."

The Clerk, who had been dozing, wakened up once more at this, and said, "She admits her guilt, m' Lud."

"You make a Qurious mistake," said the lady; " I said quilt, not guilt."

The Clerk was off to sleep again, so made no answer.

"My Lord," said the lady, "here is his heart;

I have offered it back to him often, but he always said he did not want it, he wanted mine."

So saying, she pulled out of a neat little chatelaine bag which hung at her side a small bundle wrapped up in silver paper.

" Are you willing to give it back to him ?" said Jaques.

"With all my heart," said she.

No sooner were these words uttered than a tremendous hurrah rang out from the box in which the witness was enclosed, and John Doe proved the upstart character Victoria had given him, by bursting the lid of the box open and starting up in the air, sending the ushers upon it flying, and, jumping out on the floor, he rushed up to the dock and gave the prisoner a great hug.

To this she replied by giving him a tremendous box on the ear.

" What !" said he, " did you not say you would give me all your heart with my own ?"

" Well, you have me there," said she; "but you must take the whole or none. When you asked for my heart, you asked for my hand as well, and you must take the one with the other," —giving him another box on the ear.

The curious thing was, that from each box a number of little round things fell with a clatter and scattered themselves on the floor.

The noise woke the Clerk, who, starting up, called out, " Silence in the court ! "

The hubbub still continuing, he shouted, "What is all this ? "

" Oh, nothing," said the lady, skipping out of

the dock, and administering a box on the ear to the Clerk; " only boxes of Victoria Lawsenj's."

" Lozenges !" shouted the jury. " Oh, give me some !" cried everybody.

" Certainly," said she ; and before you could count 10, the whole of the jury, counsel, ushers, and spectators were sprawling on the ground, showers of lozenges falling in all directions,—thus once more demonstrating what every one knows, that there's no rain like Victoria's, and that Royal Boxes often contain the sweet. As everybody scrambled after the lozenges, the whole court became a scene of confusion. The boys, however, who had a notion that judges must be dignified, remained quite still, only peering over their desks to see what was going on. As the boxes continued, the court got ankle-deep in lozenges, in which the people tumbled about, cramming them into their mouths and pockets by handsful. The pile rose so high that Ranulf could resist the temptation no longer, but with his long pen drew a lozenge towards him, and keeping as grave as he could, stooped down and picked it up. As he had been taught not to be selfish, he broke it in three and handed two of the pieces to Norval and Jaques. They were just going to eat them, when the lady called out—

"Oh, boys, surely you would not eat what was

picked up off the floor! that would be being bad judges of sweet things."

They stopped at once. Ranulf could not help casting a wistful eye at his bit of lozenge, but getting the better of himself, he threw it down, and the others did the same.

"That's right," said the lady; "so now you will not get a Victoria Lawsenj box on the ear, like the other stupid people tumbling about there: here are some nice clean sweetmeats for you." So saying, she handed each of the boys a lovely little box, made of chased gold and blue enamel, and marked out in diamonds on the lid, "Genuine —our own manufacture." A prompt "Thank you" came from each judge's desk; and on the boxes being opened, the boys found in them, not the common lozenges that were flying about the floor, but most lovely. bonbons, which tasted more delicious than any they ever had before.

Meanwhile the scene in court baffled description. Everybody was cramming himself with

lozenges, which, strangely enough, set them cough-
ing furiously.

" Don't you think we had better get out of this
Babel ? " said the lady.

" I think so," said Ranulf; " but how can we
do it ? "

" Oh, well," said she, " I will manage it; I will
even charge the jury, if necessary."

So saying, she took little Ranulf up in her arms,
and telling the other boys to keep close behind
her, turned and said to the jury—

" Now it is quite evident you have agreed, by
the way you are over-eating yourselves, so you
can return your verdict."

" No," said the foreman, " don't hurry us; we
are not ready."

" Oh, come, that's nonsense ; surely you can give
it *tout de suite*, after swallowing so much sugar."

" Well, we must be charged first."

" Oh, I'll charge you."

" But how ? "

" At ever so great a rate."

" Stop a minute ! " cried one.

" I seconds that motion," said another.

" The motion of seconds is too fast for minutes to be stopped ; besides, they don't belong to us, not being hours, so we have no right to stop them." So saying, she charged across the court, tumbling the jury over on the top of John Doe in the middle of the lozenges.

" Don't do that," gasped the jury, " and we will pay you whatever your charge may be."

" Oh, there's nothing to pay for the lozenges, We don't sell ourselves, we only sell other people ! Ta, ta," said the lady, and led the boys out at the door.   On reaching the entrance, she bid them good-bye, at which they looked rather blank, as they had hoped she would stay with them ; and seeing this, she said—

" My dear boys, I cannot come with you, as it is time for afternoon tea, and I must have that. T comes before U, does it not ? " So saying, she kissed them, and passed them out at the door.

As they stepped into the street a voice shouted,

"Take your seats, take your seats! Blunderbus just going off!"

The boys turned round and saw a short fat gun, evidently an infant of the Woolwich infant. On a sign on the wall opposite it was painted "DOUBLE ACTION BLUNDERBUS CO^{Y.} (unlimited)."

" Why does it point up so much?" asked Jaques.

" Well, ye see, sir, the street 'ere is pretty steep; that's how it'z erranged mortar-like."

" Which way is it going ? " asked Norval, not wishing to return by the street they had already walked along.

" Both ways," said the conductor. " Hinside passengers one way, houtside t'other."

" How do you manage that ? " asked Norval.

" Himproved happlication of Mongrieff's recoil utilizer. When we goes hoff, hinside passengers blown to Hattems, houtside recoils with shock and 'orrer in hopposite d'rection."

The boys at once resolved they would not go inside, but from curiosity ran round to look into the gun. They found, packed very tight in it, three wooden soldiers, a grate party with two brass dogs at his feet, a dancing nigger, a Miss Manage—who, being on her way to an archery meeting, had a beau by her side—a dumb-waiter, and a snob.

This reassured the boys, who, not wishing to go up the steep street towards which the gun pointed, clambered on to the top. They were scarcely seated, when a clown with a red-hot poker rushed out of the coach-office, and applied the end to the touch-hole. Immediately there is a fearful bang, and the Blunderbus starts backwards. The inside passengers fly down the street helter-skelter, except Miss Manage, who keeps herself collected, shooting out gracefully *à la* Zazel, being, alas! a sell for her beau, who wishes to cut his stick; but she, without a quiver even in her eyelid, holds on to him as he talks of flight, turning ashy pale at such a narrow escape. Not having forgotten the excellent rule to have two strings to your beau, she had made a bolt impossible.

K

The dumb-wait-
er, cured by what
would make most
people speechless
(a proof of the
truth of homœo-
pathy), flew in all
directions, shout-
ing "Yessir, yes-
sir!" The wood-

DOUBLE ACTION
BLUNDER BUS COMPANY
(UNLIMITED)

en soldiers
pulled them-
selves to-
gether for a
moment to
salute an
officer who
was passing,
which they
did with the

wrong hand, and then sped on in more fragments than before. The grate party was smashed so small that even his dogs did not know him; the nigger's nether limbs went off down the street by themselves, and were at once apprehended as black-legs by the police, while the rest of him formed a kind of Black's Atlas upon the pavement. The snob, as was natural, disappeared in any number of vulgar fractions.

The Blunderbus ran back at a great pace for a mile, butting over two Papal bulls, sending spin-ning mules without number, and ended by knock-ing ten feet out of a square yard, in which a regi-ment of soldiers was being drilled.

Our trio, who had been rather alarmed du-ring their ride, jumped off the gun the mo-ment it stopped, and, as boys will always do, ran off to look at the soldiers. On getting near they were surprised to see that each man had a nigger lady beside him. While they were wondering what this could mean, the Colonel, who wore a shell jacket, and had a husky voice, rode up on a clothes-horse, and handed Norval a parade state, which was as follows :—

TWOTY-TENTH BOSHSHIRE RUFFS, 37th *Marchuary* 7718.					
	Present with Leave.	Present without Leave.	Absent in Mind.	Absent in Body.	Tea Tottles.
Kernels, . .	o	1½	1½	o	
Ragers, . . .	o	2¾	2	¾	
Catpins, . . .	o	7.09	5	2.09	
Bluelandlords,	o	10	10	o	
Scar Gents, .	o	15.4	o	15.4	
Noodlers, . .	o	11	11	o	
Fank and Rile,	o	550.7	550.7	o	
T Tottles, .	Add	them up	for your	self.	

A. NUTT,
Kernel of the Core.

" How is it," said practical Jaques, who observed that the men had only wooden guns, "that your men have no rifles ? "

"Well, sir, we don't go in for new-fangled notions here," said the Colonel; "we hold on to our Brown Bessies, as you see."

All the nigger ladies grinned tremendously at this, and called out, "Ya! ya! dat all right, Massa Kurnel."

" Will you keep those brown Bessiers stock-still ? " shouted the Colonel to the men; " if you don't, you shan't have any ball."

At this everybody looked very blank, and the Brown Bessies became suddenly immovable. The Colonel then gave the word of command—

" Boshshire Roughs,

'SHUN."

All the men at once turned away, and put their hands in their pockets, displaying the most con-temptuous indifference to the brown ladies, who now were all attention and smiles, trying to coax the men to turn to them again.

"Will you inspect the corps?" said the Colonel.

The boys walked down to the end of the line, whereupon the band, which consisted of one fife and 29 triangles, struck up—

Tinkle, tinkle, little Shah,
* Did you ever see a nigger with a white papa?
Pickaninny here and pickaninny da,
    You'll never find a single darkey, ha, ha, ha!

As they came near the line, the Colonel took from his pocket a magnifying-glass as big as the crown of a hat, and handed it to Norval, who asked—

"What am I to do with it?"

At this question the entire regiment burst into a tremendous guffaw, laughing till the tears ran down their cheeks, and the whole line was a scene of pocket-handkerchiefs, each being as big as a Turkish-bath towel, and as there was a high wind, of course this caused a great fluttering and shaking. The boys thought this very unlike the soldiers they had been accustomed to see, particularly as the officers and sergeants laughed and

shook more than the men, and the Colonel, going
off into a broad grin, laughed and grew so fat that
his very steed became infected, and losing half

its understanding and all its breeding, indulged
in a horse-laugh, which shook it so that when the
rider fattened, it sank under his weight, bringing
him plump to the ground.   A fatigue party had
tŏ come to his assistance, and when he had been
propped up by two long crutches, one on each

side of his horse, he tried to speak, but could scarcely get on for laughing.

" You want, ha, ha, ha! to know, ho, ho, ho! what the big glass is for ? "

" Yes."

" Well, you see, ah, ha, ha, ha! it's because of, ha, ha, ha, ha! Mr Sadpebble and Lord Guardsell."

" Who are they ? "

" Oh! they, ha, ha, ha! were the mime primister and skekentary of skate for raw, ho, ho, ho!"

" But what have they to do with the glass ? "

" They managed things so, you see, ha, ha, aha, ha, ha! that everything was getting small, ho, ho, ho! the regiments were getting smaller, and the men were getting smaller, and the chests were getting smaller, and the efficiency was getting smaller, and the contentment was getting smaller, ha, ha, ha, ha! so they, ha, ha! they, ha, ha, ha! they, ah, ha, ha, ha! they took to military spectacles to make things look better."

" But surely no one would be deceived by that ? "

" Oh yes, ha, ha, ha ! they deceived the general."

" Which general ? " said Jaques.

" Oh, we've only one general here—General Public—he's the boy for mobilisation, oh, haha, haha, ha ! "

He laughed so loud and shook so much that the crutches, trembling under him, stuck in the ground, and his horse, walking off, left him up in the air between the crutches. This did not seem to disconcert him at all, but brandishing his sword, he shouted—

" Battalion, halt ! "

As the regiment was standing still already, the boys thought this a very funny order to give; but they were more surprised still when they saw the whole line set off marching, all limping as if they had blistered feet.

" Very well, *very* steadily done," said the Colonel, as they came bobbing and limping towards him, like a lot of ducks in a thunder-storm. Presently, on their coming close to him, he shouted—

" Double ! "

At this they all turned round and went off in the opposite direction, limping slower and slower.

" Surely that's wrong," said Jaques ; " that's right about turn ; they should have gone straight on and faster."

" Not at all," said the Colonel ; " in our movements we follow Levrett's manœuvres."

" But that's not the way to double march," said Jaques.

" Oh yes, it is. Did you ever see a March hare double ? Well, we double just as he does. Pussian tactics, you know."

Without waiting for an answer he cried—

" Discharge ! "

and gallantly going at the head of his men on his crutches, shouted " Victory ! " After they were brought to a stand at one end of the ground, he gave the order—

" Stand a tease ! "

Upon this the Brown Bessies turned round upon the men and began to plague them most horribly, pulling their hair, poking fingers into their ears, and pricking them with pins. The men

stood it for some time wonderfully, but at last began to bawl out.

"No bawl practice without my orders!" shouted the Colonel; and then tremendously loud—

"ALL DRESS!"

Everybody immediately stopped. The Brown Bessies at once produced combs and brushes, and commenced a vigorous hair-dressing, and the men began putting on white kid-gloves.

"What is the meaning of that?" said Ranulf.

" Preparing for ball practice," said the Colonel.
" In our tactics we go in for leading the enemy a
pretty dance.   That's far the best way."

" Change ranks ! "

he shouted.   The boys could not afterwards make
out how it had happened, but the Colonel had
scarcely given this order when, instead of being on
the dull, dingy parade-ground, they stood on a most
lovely floor that seemed all to be made of ivory
inlaid with gold.   The Brown Bessies were brown
no longer, but fair ladies beautifully dressed ; the
men were in splendid costumes ; the band had no
triangles, but discoursed most lovely music.   The
boys, looking round, saw they were in an immense
hall, lighted by ten thousand wax candles ; and
as all the walls were mirror, the brilliant scene
repeated itself as far as the eye could see,
and probably further.   But the most beautiful
thing of all was, that when the ladies and gentlemen began to dance, instead of bouncing about in
a crowd, bumping and knocking one another,
each couple floated from the ground, gliding along

in the air smoothly and gracefully; and as the music rose and fell, fast and then slow, they flew, now in joyous bounds, now gracefully circling in soft dreamy waves, now whirling with birdlike speed, anon wafted along like a gossamer borne on the almost motionless air of a summer day; the measure having always such grace and ease in its fury, such firm-swept curve in its calm, that the little fellows stood gazing in rapt delight.

When the dance was over, half the mirrors on the walls folded back, moved by unseen hands, and the ladies and gentlemen strolled out to a lovely terrace, rich with flowers of every hue, where fountains threw water in sparkling diamonds to the sun. As each couple emerged from the building, a flower that grew on the parterre detached a lovely blossom, which, floating in the air towards them, growing ever larger and larger, moved wherever they turned their steps, shading them from the sun, and surrounding them with its perfume. Strange, too, that it did not appear to be matter of chance which flower performed this friendly office, for the blossom that floated over the heads of each pair that roamed the garden, was always of a colour harmonising admirably with the costume beneath. A couple dressed in pale blue were attended by a primrose; two that wore green had a lovely snow-white lily for their shade; a third pair, who were in white, rejoiced in the protection of a scarlet geranium; and a fourth, in a pearly grey, had a most delicate pink blossom for their attendant.

It was a lovely sight, but small boys soon get tired of the beautiful unless there is some fun going; so after our trio had gazed for a time on the people with their varied dresses, they began to long for something more exciting. Looking about, they saw at one end of the lawn a large gateway, and started off at a run to see whither it led. On getting near the gate, they observed a funny little man sitting on the arch above it, who, the moment they came up, said, "Put them down."

"We don't carry anything," said Norval.

"Yes you do, though," said the little man. "What names do you bear?"

The boys told him, at which he gave a triumphant sniff, and said, "If you bear names, look at your dictionary and see what bear means. My dictionary says it means carry. Don't carry them any longer; put them down."

"What is he up to?" said Jaques, bewildered.

"Up to the top of the door, don't you see, stoopid?" said the little man. "Sometimes I'm up to anything, but just at present I'm only up to the top of a door. Why do you make me a contradiction of myself?"

"But we don't," said Norval.

"Oh yes, you do. Here I am up at the top of the door, and yet you make me be down upon you at the same time. It's very inconvenient to be put in two places at once; so don't do it again, that's all."

"But you can't be in two situations at once," said Jaques.

"But I say you can," said the little man, "and more than two. You can be in the heat of an argument, in the middle of a cold audience, in the wrong box, and in the hope of getting out of it, and in a great mistake in thinking so, all at once. So once more I say, put them down."

"But what are we to put down, and where are we to put them, whatever they may be?" said Norval.

"Didn't I say your names (everybody visiting towers should put down their names)? and where would you think of putting names down but in a book, I should like to know?" said the little man.

"But where is the book?" said Jaques; "I don't see any."

"Oh, most ill-informed little boy! in the visitors' book, to be sure."

" But where is it ? "

" You know that best. Surely you know where your own book is ? "

" But you said the visitors' book."

" Well, and are you not a visitor? so if you put it down in your book it will be in the visitor's book, won't it ? "

This seemed to be nothing short of downright nonsense to the boys ; but to please the little man, they took out their pocket-books, and gravely wrote their own names in them.

" Now, let me see," said the little man, producing a pair of spectacles with eyes as big as saucers.

They held up their books, and the little man took a glance through his spectacles. The moment he saw the writing he gave a start of surprise and disgust, and nearly tumbled off his perch.

" Woe is me !" he exclaimed, wringing his hands. " Is this the effect of Education Acts and School Boards ? Why, they are upside up, when I told you it was down they were to be."

L

"But they are down in the book," said Norval.

"No," said the little man, sorrowfully, "they are not even that. They are up at the very top of the page, all of them. Oh dear! it upsets me completely," he added, as, bending down, he raised his legs in the air and stood upon his head.

"Ah, now," he said, "it is all right! they are down now. You see if I were standing on cere- mony I could not have let you pass, but standing on my head heals up the difficulty. It's a pate-nt way of my own. Now you may pass on."

"But the gate is not open," said Jaques.

"Well, open it," said the little man.

"But we have not got a key."

"Well, then, if you have not got A key, try the key of B."

Jaques looked puzzled, and said, "I don't under- stand."

"There," said the little man, pointing to a rope attached to the bolt of the gate—"you're A flat; B E sharp now, and C what F-ect ten or a dozen treble G-erks applied altogether to the bar at the base there may have in the D-velopment of a passage."

This speech made the boys look at one another, and laugh. "Well," said the little man, "passages generally do open with a chord seem funny as it may; so just try."

At this, Norval seized the rope, and, tugging it vigorously, the gate swung slowly on its hinges.

"Ah! what lovely opening bars!" cried the little man, beating time with one leg; "there never was a passage better done on the P an' O."

The remark may be made here, in passing, that a match against time with both legs is common, but to beat time with one leg! extraordinary feat!!! The passage must have been very legato, or it could not have been done.

When the gate was fully open, the boys all said, "Thank you."

"Oh, never mind thanking me; it's been a case of stuck-at-a passage long enough; get through it in treble quick time, and be happy.'

No second bidding was needed, and the little fellows, running through the gateway, found themselves in a courtyard in which stood a high tower, whose stones looked like transparent green glass, and the lines between them as if raspberry-jam had been used for lime.

After looking at it for a few moments, Jaques exclaimed, " I wonder what the tower is for ? "

" Nothing at all at present, thank you ; I'm not 'ungry," replied a *forte* voice, in somewhat stony accents.

" Why, it can speak," cried Jaques, quite astonished.

" Of course I can. If 'ouses may talk, why should not I ? "

" But houses don't talk," said Ranulf.

" 'Ouses don't talk, don't they ? Ha, ha, ha ! " shouted the tower, till its sides shook so that the boys were afraid it would tumble, and its tiers would have fallen, only they had not the cheek to run down. " Ha, ha, ha, ha ! So you think 'ouses can't talk. Now I've 'eard it said they talk too much. Look at the 'Ouse of Commons, and you'll see that you never made a Biggar mistake; it seems to do nothing but talk."

"Ah, but," said Jaques, "that's different; it's not a great high stone thing, like you."

"Not stone, and not 'igh! Is that all you know? Isn't a glad stone always getting up in it, and ain't the dizzy 'ights at the top? But I shan't talk to you hany more."

"Why not, please?" said Jaques, timidly.

"Why not! you are not a purpose, nor a heffect, nor a hend,—are you?"

"No," said Jaques.

"Then I shan't talk to you. When I talk I always talk to some purpose, or to some heffect, or to some hend. I like the last best. Give me some hend to talk to, and I'll talk no hend."

"Some end of what?" asked Norval; "is it the end of a stick, or a cigar, or what?"

"Oh, to the hend of time, or hanything. Make a hend of yourself, and you will see how I'll talk to you then.'

The boys did not quite see that to be the talk of a tower was a sufficient temptation to suicide, so remained silent.

" Well, I'm glad, at all hevents, you've made a hend of something ; making a hend of speaking is better than making a hend of nothing. Now that you've made a hend, I can talk to it, if you will promise that the hend will attend to the hend, that the hend in view may in the hend be brought to a hend, and that——"

" Why," said Norval, interrupting, " I beg your pardon, but you said you would talk no end, and it seems to me it is all end together."

At this the tower completely forgot itself, indeed went off into a towering passion, and stormed away for ever so long. Some people may think that it is strange a tower should storm itself, instead of being stormed ; but the fact was that its mortar being ill tempered, it exploded spontaneously. The way in which a tower flies into a passion is very difficult to describe, and it will not be attempted here. Suffice it to say, that of course it used its wings.   Its rage was so great as to make it speechless, which, from the rubbish it had been talking on end before, was just as well, for though it kept on end, it did so silently. The boys began to walk round it, and on getting to the other side, they found a very low door, over which was a large placard :—

VISITORS
WHO HAVE
NO VIEWS OF THEIR OWN
WILL FIND SOME
AT THE TOP OF THIS TOWER.

Those who change their views charged extra.

FRAMES OF MIND FOR THE VIEWS MAY BE HAD AT MODERATE PRICES. .

ADMISSION FREE.
ON WHOLEYDAYS HALF-PRICE.

N.B.—*Whatever goes in at the bottom must come out at the top.*

By Order.

A. B. FEATER,

Custodier.

Now "must" is a word that people are constantly telling little boys not to use, but are just as constantly using themselves in speaking to them.   Accordingly it is not very surprising that when boys see the word "must" painted up in large letters, they should feel inclined to resist. When Norval, and Jaques, and Ranulf saw "must go out at the top" on the placard, their bump of combativeness at once became irritated ; and, after a short conference, they resolved they would go into the tower, and would not go out at the top.   Norval's idea was that there was some one inside to catch anybody that entered, and force him to the top, so he told Jaques and Ranulf that he would peep in, if they would be ready to pull him back should any one try to take hold of him. He then advanced cautiously, and put his head in at the door.   The moment he did so, he called out—

"OH HOLD ME!"

The "oh" was very loud, but the "hold"

sounded more distant, and the "me" was so far off as to be difficult to hear. Jaques and Ranulf held on stoutly to Norval's legs, but found they could not haul him out, though pulling with all their might. While they were still struggling, Norval's voice behind them said, "It's no use, you had better let them go." On looking round they were amazed to see Norval's head upside down just at their backs, hanging by a long neck, not thicker than a sausage, from the top of the tower.

In ordinary circumstances this would have shocked them horribly, but then wonders began to come almost as matters of course, and Norval's head drooping down like a ball at the end of a string had such an irresistibly comical appearance, that they both burst into a loud fit of laughter, in which Norval himself joined most heartily. But when they had enjoyed their laugh, and began to look matters and Norval in the face, the puzzle was what to do; for they saw that to resist going out at the top would be useless, and feared that if Norval's legs were released, his body would go out at the top and be smashed. After thinking a little, Jaques asked Ranulf for his top-cord, proposing to tie it to Norval's legs, and let him down quietly. "Oh, but," said Ranulf, "the cord would never reach so far."

"Oh yes," said Jaques; "don't you see that whatever goes in at the bottom must come out at the top? so the string will get long if we hold it, just as Norval's neck did." This proved to be correct; for on tying the cord to Norval's legs and letting them go, they flew up at once, and Jaques and Ranulf holding on prevented Norval tumbling over. But while Jaques was easing the cord down, by moving his hands forward, he thoughtlessly brought them within the doorway, when at once his arms flew up the tower, and Norval had in his turn to assist Ranulf to hold Jaques, whose hands shot out at the top of the tower, and hung down behind them as Norval's head had done before. Norval and Ranulf began to get the cord ready to let Jaques down safely in his turn,

but Jaques (mechanical again) relieved them from
the trouble by making use of his long arms. He
seized each of his heels firmly in one hand, and
bidding the other boys let go, eased his body
gently up the tower, out at the top, and down to
the ground, and then drew his hands out. The
sight of him, with his monstrous arms, produced
another burst of laughter, which increased when
Jaques, wanting to give Ranulf a box on the
ear * for laughing, found that his hand, instead
of touching him, flew into a rhododendron bush
ever so far down the garden-walk. Although
neither he nor his brother could shorten their
drawn-out members to their original size, still
these were so far elastic, that they could draw
them in to about half their enormous length, and
throw them out again as they pleased. After
they had experimented a little with their un-
wieldy projections, making them perform all sorts
of antics, so that the three screamed with laugh-

* In fun, of course. These boys had learned what all boys
should learn, never to get angry at being laughed at.

ter, Norval took
it into his head
that he would like
to have a look into
the tower; for on
his previous jour-
ney through it, he
had been so hur-
ried that he saw
nothing — in fact,
had gone through

like winking. He therefore raised his head, drawing in his long neck, till he and the tower looked like a gigantic pewter pot with its handle. On getting his nose to the edge, he at once exclaimed, " Oh, what a jolly smell!" This excited Ranulf's curiosity, so he at once rushed to the door to have a sniff, and to make sure he was not caught as his brothers had been, he took care not to put even his hands in at the door. But unfortunately he forgot the slightly Roman tendency of his nose, which, as he tried to get a whiff of the scent, flew up the tower, nearly poking out Norval's eye at the top, and ran down the outside to the ground. Ranulf, who did not like having his nose pulled in this fashion, was just going to cry, but remembering the fairy's caution, exclaimed to himself, " Not if I knows it," pulled out his handkerchief, and turning round gently did as boys usually do when they have had to gulp down a sob.

" Now, then, get on," cried Jaques.

" But what shall I do?" said Ranulf.

" Do! follow your nose, to be sure. Why
don't you come down by your bridge ? "

" What bridge ? "

" Why, the bridge of your nose. I'll hold it
steady for you."

Jaques accordingly seized Ranulf's nose in his
long arms, and giving it a hitch round the lightning-conductor at the top of the tower, held the
end slanting, making it hang like the rope for
the terrific ascents of tight-rope performers, and
down this improvised bridge Ranulf slid success-
fully to the ground, after which Jaques removed
the hitch from the lightning-conductor, and Ranulf,
who had a taste for the sea, coiled his nose neatly
upon the ground, like a hawser on board ship, and
taking the coils in his hand, threw them over his
shoulder. His brothers seeing this, stowed away
their slack also, and had scarcely done so, when
there was a tremendous flourish of trumpets, and
a being that might have passed for a pantaloon,
as he was clothed entirely in golden trouser-legs
(the Blunderland substitute for coats of arms)

entered the gate. In reality he was a herald, although you would not have guessed it, as he wore no ruff round his throat. Behind him strode six stalwart trumpeters, each of whom, instead of blowing his own trumpet—as is too common nowadays — held his instrument to the mouth of his left-hand neighbour. There was an awkwardness about this arrangement, however, for the man at the right end of the line had no trumpet for his mouth, and the man at the other end had no mouth for his trumpet. But in Blunderland, difficulties which elsewhere would be thought insurmountable are soon overleapt. Accordingly, the sixth trumpet was managed thus: The moment the others were raised, trumpeter No. 1, who had no instrument, looked hard along the line, and called out, "No. 6, you be blowed!" and as obedience is the rule in Blunderland, as opposed to what occurs elsewhere, this command was quite enough to make trumpet No. 6 tootle-ootle away as loud as the rest.

It seemed to be the business of these trumpeters to make as much noise as they could whenever the unfortunate herald opened his lips to make his proclamation.   The sort of thing that went on was this : The herald, having unrolled his paper, cleared his throat, of which there was much need ; for if there was no ruff outside, that was more than could be said of the interior.   If he had had colera he could not have been more nekroky.* Having given a hem, long enough to go round the skirt of a lady's dress, even of modern proportions, he began to read—

    " Roy——"

Instantly his thread was broken by tra ta ta, ti ta ta, tatata ta tum, tatatraratatata, from all the trumpets at once.

    Another attempt to go on—

    " —al."

    Tra ta t't't'a, t't'a—tra ta ta ti ta ti tati ta tum ta tum ta, ta, ta.

---

    * Perhaps the small reader does not understand.   Let him wait till he begins Greek.

When this had happened over and over again, the tra-ta-ta-ing getting louder and longer each time, the herald calmly sat down on the ground, laid aside his proclamation, produced from his pocket a gilt bladder, which he quietly proceeded to blow up till it was full of air, and fastened to the end of his baton by a string about a foot long. Having carefully tested its strength by giving it a few thumps on the ground, he rose, and recommenced reading his proclamation. Instantly behind him began once more the braying of trumpets; but before one tra-ta could escape, bang, b'ng, b'ng, b'ng, bang, bang came the bladder down upon the heads of the six trumpeters. This stopped five of the too-toos * coming from them,

---

* If any one, with a mind not delivered from the bondage of mere vulgar arithmetic, should object that two 2's make 4, and not 5, we have only to say that we don't care a fraction, and refuse to alter our addition for any such common multiple of a fellow. If any other spelling B-ound individual should say that "toos" is not according to English orthography, we beg to remind him that Eng means narrow, and we prefer to go in for all abroad in such matters; and this being a book of fun, we adopt the funnytick mode.

M

the whole six trumpeters being knocked out of
time.   But as there was nobody to take the blow
for No. 6 trumpet, it was brazen enough to go on
all by itself, as if it would be blowed if it would
stop.   The herald, however, evidently knew what
he was about, for he ran to No. 6 trumpet and
gave it such a blowing up, up its mouth, that
nothing could get out for ever so long; indeed
the air was too much for it, and it could not give
it off even in parts; as for the bass, it could not
get so low; treble X ecution was quite as impossible; the third part was ten or more notes beyond
it; and the only remaining one was altogether so.

Having thus succeeded in obtaining silence, the
herald proceeded to read his proclamation, and
got through some lines before the trumpeters
recovered sufficiently to commence their noise
once more; when seeing them about to begin,
he repeated the bang bang bang, bang bang, process with most excellent effect—and making about
fifteen pauses to perform this operation, he managed to read the whole.   In order not to try the

reader's patience, it is thought better to give it without the interrupting bangs—in fact, bang off.

By the King—

A Proclamation.

WHEREAS it is our will and desire to maintain a clear course, so that we may be kept placed in the races of the earth, and that our people may continue to have a handy capacity for all athletic sports, likewise to avert the risk of the mussels of our subjects getting limp at the end of our royal line by any shellfish a'baiting (after the barb'rous manner of the fishy policy of the Angles) of the care bestowed by it on generations yet unborn—

We have thought it would fit, with or without the advice of our Prating Council, and the Cakes of our Parliament, to appoint and declare, and we do hereby, by and with, or passing by and without the said advice, appoint and declare, that immediately, or even sooner, all who hear or do not hear of this proclamation, shall assemble without delay on a spot to be fixed by us at some future time, there to hold our annual games.

And our will and pleasure further is, that prizes be awarded to those of our subjects who display the greatest skill in performing any of the following feats of agility and strength :—

   I. Running up a bill with spears and ponds.
  II. Taking a spring from a well in dancing pumps.
 III. Carrying 6 Woolwich infants in an estimate.
  IV. Handling a weighty argument, and hurling it at an adversary.
   V. Knocking down a five-storey house by one blow of a hammer at the bidding of the purchaser.
  VI. Carrying a measure with a Committee sitting upon it through two Houses.
 VII. Keeping a gentleman in your eye when you have a stye in it already.
VIII. Carrying a crowded house along with you for three hours.
  IX. Running a tremendous risk, and beating it.
   X. Keeping time for the human race.
       And such others as we may appoint.

GIVEN AT OUR COURT AT LUCKINGHAM ON THE 32ND OF APRIL 8177, IN THE ONE HUNDRED AND THIRTY-NINTH YEAR OF OUR REIGN.

The herald having completed the reading of the proclamation, evidently expected that, the proper time having now arrived, his trumpeters would blow a vigorous flourish, as in duty bound; but instead of this there was dead silence, all the trumpeters standing stock-still, with their hands hanging at their sides, and mouths wide open. At this the herald got white with passion, the choler

rose so at his throat that he could bear it no longer, but cut up rough, the cuffs flying from him in showers, till at last he burst the bladder with

a terrific bang on the nose of No. 1, who took
no more notice than if he had been made of
gutta-percha. The herald calmed down as suddenly as he had flared up, and after looking at the
motionless figures for a moment, quietly remarked,
" Oh, I'm in no hurry, I can wait," produced from
the pocket of one of his many trouser-legs a copy
of ' Enquire within upon Everything '—a book
much studied in Blunderland—and commenced
reading, evidently in the hope that he might in
course of time come upon a receipt that would
enable him to settle the hash of his saucy attendants. The trumpeters could have borne any
amount of violence, but the herald's tactics were
too much for them; so before he could get his
spectacles adjusted to commence reading, they
all placed their trumpets to their mouths, and
blew a most elegant tootle-ootle, at which the
herald, smiling sweetly, turned and said, " Thanks,
thanks, my children!" and producing a box from
another pocket, handed each of them a stick of
barley-sugar. Now no one will think it surpris-

ing that the sight of a free distribution of barley-sugar should be rather exciting to three small

boys like our heroes. And although they had been well taught that little men should not thrust themselves on people to ask for things, still, being in Blunderland, it is not strange that they should be a little infected by the character of the country, and do what would have been not at all good manners anywhere else. So Jaques, taking advantage of his long arms, unwound one of them, and passing it round to the back of the trumpeters, thrust it out between two of them. The herald, quite unsuspecting, placed in it a stick of barley-sugar, when it was instantly withdrawn, and Jaques handed the barley-sugar to his elder brother. Repeating the process, he succeeded in getting sticks for Ranulf and for himself, the

herald being in great astonishment, as he found
that though he had given out more than six
sticks, and the trumpeters were all sucking away
furiously, there was always an empty hand
stretched out from some quarter or another for
more. Looking behind the trumpeters, all he
could see was what he took to be a garden water-
ing-pipe lying on the ground, but which was in
reality Jaques' arm. Not to be beaten, he muttered
to himself that he would go on till he found it
out; so, to the boys' great delight, kept putting
sticks into Jaques' hand, until his box was empty
and their pockets full. They felt, however, when
all was over, that while it might not be of great
consequence, still, to be little gentlemen as they
ought, they must not leave matters unexplained;
so, after a short consultation how it was to be
done, Jaques' hand again appeared between the
trumpeters holding all the sticks of barley-sugar,
minus one little bit that Ranulf, with a haste ex-
cusable at six years, but no longer, had nibbled
off, and a voice behind the herald said, " Please

sir, may we have them?" Turning round, he saw the three boys, and gazing at them with their coils, exclaimed in amazement—

"Why, you must be three rolls of endless wax-taper out for a walk!"

"Oh no; we aren't tapirs," said Ranulf, who, having a recollection of a beast with a long snout in his animals-book, thought this was a reflection on his nose. He felt very much inclined to put his fingers to it; but a sense of propriety, and a difficulty in finding the point of it among the folds, combined to restrain him.

"Then if you're not tapers," said the herald, "you must be sons of a gun, built on the coil system—Armstrong's patent, eh? or perhaps you are in the still line?"

"Nurse never thinks so," said Jaques. "She says she would like to see a little more of the still about us — that we are too full of good spirits."

"And what is the still business for, except to produce good spirits; but," said the herald, sud-

denly assuming a tremendous air of official dignity, "we must tarry no longer; the games are
about to commence."

"Oh, but please, sir, may we keep the barley-
sugar?"

"Yes," said he, and was going to add "but"
something, only he did not get time, for his Yes
was instantly followed by three Thank-yous, and
three enormous bites at the barley-sugar.

"Stop, stop, stop!" he cried. "I thought you
wanted to keep it."

The boys knew that they should not speak with
their mouths full; and having as much in them
as good manners allow, they were compelled to
nod.

"And how can you both eat your lollypop and
keep it? There's a poser for you," said the
herald, folding his arms, throwing back his head,
and planting his right foot forward in a manner
which plainly meant, "I poses for a reply."

It was a poser in one way, for no answer could

be given to it by nod or shake; and as the mouths were still full, it remained unanswered, the boys wavering between—

"Speak when you are spoken to"

and

"Don't speak with your mouth full."

The herald's notion of his own dignity seemed to be greatly increased by there being apparently no answer to his question, which was just as well, for as he got full of importance he got empty of everything else (on the well-known principle of natural philosophy, that two things cannot occupy the same space at the same time), and so forgot all about his question.

While he was still posing, a mounted disorderly galloped on to the ground, shouting—

"Here, hi, hollo, you there! What's yer name? How long d'ye mean to keep the king waiting?"

In a moment all the herald's dignity was gone. He trembled till his trouser-legs were fluttering all round him, like a cock's feathers when he shakes himself, and cried—

" The king waiting ! oh, oh dear ! " gathered his trouser-legs about him, and fled through the gateway, like an old woman running in a shower of rain.

The trumpeters, thus relieved of the dread of the gilded bladder, blew a tremendous flourish, threw their trumpets in the air, and then the end

one giving a back, they set off in leap-frog after the herald.

The boys made after them as fast as they could, soon outstripping them with their young legs, and on passing through the gate found the people assembled for the games. It was indeed a lovely sight. Unlike such gatherings among those who do not blunder, there were no thimble-riggers; no dismal niggers; no men with two black cards and a red; no shouts of four to one, bar one; no little girls with careworn faces and work-worn tights, faded and patched, performing on stilts to a consumptive drum and a time-defy-ing flageolet; no display of paint, false hair, and falser smiles; no pouring in of sparkling gooseberry; no pouring out of wild and wicked words; no reeling and staggering; no shouting and brawling; no fingers in other people's pockets, and fists in other people's eyes. Such things are only to be witnessed in countries where the people have grown out of the condition of blundering, and have reached an advanced stage of civilisa-tion and intelligence. Here in this yet unen-lightened country things were quite different. The sight was lovely. The ladies and gentlemen whom the boys had seen before on the lawn,

were here assembled, along with a host of other
people of humbler rank, the rich costumes of
the ladies and gentlemen contrasting with the
less costly dresses of the lower classes, grouped
as they were with the most charming harmony
and accommodation of colours too beautiful for
description, forming a sight never to be forgotten. The effect was made still more charming by
the flowers that had sheltered the groups on the
lawn being formed into a vast sun-shade above
—a gigantic white lily, with its bell turned down-
wards, being the centre, and the circles going
out from it in the most delicate gradations of
colour through all the tints of the rainbow; the
edges of this gigantic and gorgeous *ombrelle*
being formed of enormous bright fern-leaves,
the points of which, bending towards the ground,
were by some unseen means kept gently waving,
wafting the air charged with the fragrance of
the flowers in delicious coolness over the whole
assemblage.

In rather incongruous contrast to the elegance

and luxurious refinement of the scene was the conduct of one individual, who, although he had a crown on his head, was rushing about with an apron on and a napkin under his arm, carrying dishes and bottles in all directions.

" *Waiter !* " shouted a voice on one side.

The King. " Yessir."

" Four sausage rolls, a hice, and three pops."

The King. " Yessir."

" *Waiter !* " cried another.

The King. " Yessir."

" Two 'alfs 'alf-and-'alf, an' 'alf a sandwich."

The King. " Yessir."

" *Waiter !* " roared a third.

The King. " Yessir."

"Cold beef and pickles, two brandies, and a split."

The King. " Yessir."

"Come along, king," said a fourth, "attend to the comforts of your subjects."

The King. " Yessir."

" Two churchwardens and a screw of tobacco."

The King. " Yessir."

The poor king did his very best, and rushed about most energetically.   He managed, like a good waiter, to keep up a considerable fire of chaff.   A man having offered him a tip of 2s. 6d., he exclaimed, " Oh, sir, you cannot give a king less than a crown!"   To a party who gave him 15s., he objected, " This won't do, sir; I must have five more."

" Why ? "

" Three crowns is the Pope's allowance.   It takes four to make a real sovereign, sir."

But although trying to be as merry and lively as possible, he found it very hard work, and the moment the herald appeared, dropped his napkin, six plates of lamb and salad and eight pewter pots he was carrying, tore off his apron, changed a crown, and picking up his robe of state and  his sceptre and ball, gave a royal wave of his hand.

The herald was at once seized and brought forward, and, addressing him, the king said, " What, ho, thou caitiff! say, how hast thou dared so long to keep thy sovereign waiting ? "

If the herald had been a log, he could not have remained more stolidly immovable. There was dead silence for a few moments, and then the king again spoke, " 'Tis well thou knowest thou shouldest not dare to answer back to a king, for this is half thine offence pardoned. Canst thou bring forward anything why punishment should not overtake thee for the other half ? " At this

N

the herald did bring something forward, for he brought up one hand, and placing the thumb to the end of his nose, he slowly extended the

fingers as far out as he could, and waggled them about, then he placed the thumb of the other hand to the little finger already stretched out, and extending his other fingers, waggled them too. The boys were aghast at thus seeing a subject making a long nose at a king, and still more when he finished by bringing his hand sharply up against his open mouth, producing a sound like the popping of a well-fitted cork.

The king, however, seemed not at all struck in the way they were by the herald's conduct, but turning to an attendant said, " Bring forward the whys man, that we may get the interpretation of these heraldic emblems."

The whys man was, as might have been expected, the querist man that ever was seen. Nobody could fail to see that he was a man of mark of interrogation, for when you looked at him you saw a great deal of curl at the head, and when you reached his feet he came to a stop.*

"Your Majesty, come and I obey," said the seer.

The boys thought this bad grammar, and very rude on the part of a subject (not knowing that he meant, "Command, I obey"); for, as Norval said to Jaques, a subject giving dictation, instead of a subject being given in dictation, was contrary to all their school experience. But they were beginning not to be surprised at anything.

"Didst thou behold the mysterious signs just

*. If anybody should think, on reading this, that the statement is superfluous, because all men come to a stop at their feet, he will please remember that men often have more sole under their feet than anywhere else : in fact, they are so fond of fishy and slippery ways that they always go upon soles and eels ; and some of them are so fast, that so far from stopping at their feet, they go such lengths that they stop at nothing.

made by our herald ?   What mean they ?" said
the king.

" Will your Majesty deign to say whether you
desire to be answered with rhyme and reason or
without rhyme or reason ? "

" Whichever seemeth best unto thee, oh seer ! "

" Then, seriously speaking, I would say that if
a point of view be taken, such as those who take
points of view, with a view to getting the point of
view, that brings best into view the true view of
the point, which ought to be kept in view, in the
view of getting at the point——"

" Oh, stop, stop, stop ! " cried the king ; " which
is that—' with ' or ' without ' ? "

" ' Without,' sire," answered the seer.

" Then, for pity's sake, let us have with, if it will
save us from being compassed with so many
points.   I feel pricked all over."

Your Majesty shall be obeyed,
Although in sooth I am afraid,
A pointless rhyme is not the thing
To lay before so great a king.

You fain would know why herald's nose
By aid of fingers longer grows,
And why by slap upon his mug
He makes a hollow sound like " jug."
Methinks he by these signs would say,
'Twas well he stayed so long away.
By sound of cork he first would tell,
How waiting long, you waited well.
Fired by desire for subjects' weal,
You ran about with plates of veal
And ham, hot kidneys, bottled stout;
In short, you wildly flew about,
The slave of all, though monarch great,
Good lesson in the cares of state.
He next the royal attention draws,
To all the tips on nose and paws,
By which he plainly means to in
dicate how 'twould have been a sin
Had he by quick return to you
Deprived you of the tips you drew,
While you were waiting on your p-
eople drawing corks and serving tea.
Indeed he'd say, by him your pop
ularity is now tip-top.
He therefore claims a pardon free.
The seer hath spoken.

" Fiddle-dee-dee!" cried the king; " to such de-
fence I cannot listen.   It may be with rhyme, but

is certainly without reason. If it comes to anything it comes to this, that he kept me waiting so
long in order that I might get tips, eh ?   That
is seeking to give the king the sack.   I would
be mad ere I accepted such a mumm sham peni-
tence.   I declare it brand'ed as a shabbily-con-
cocted whine; so turn from it, and laugh it to
scorn.   He shall have his mead.   Summon the
headsman, and let him whisk it off.

The executioner at once appeared, set his
block in front of the throne, felt the edge of his
axe, advanced to the herald, and began to drag
him forward.

"Friend," said the herald (he had turned quaker
at the sight of the block), "why dost thou draw
this way ? "

" Because my business is funny cuts," said the
executioner, giving him a sudden pull.

" Don't ketch me up so if thou art a Jack in the
box wood way ; thou shouldst not put such hard
lines on a fellow."

"I call you rather knave than fellow," replied the

executioner, getting somewhat surly, " I don't need you to tell me how to make the cuts on my block."

The boys began to feel rather uncomfortable at

the idea of seeing a head cut off. They were somewhat relieved, however, to notice that the executioner and attendants, on getting the herald to the block, did not apply his neck to it, but made him sit down. They then began searching among the many trouser-legs that hung behind him, and were so long at this operation that

Jaques, who, being a schoolboy, had an impression of his own as to what they were after, suddenly exclaimed—

"Instead of fumbling that way, why don't you take dow—— "

But care-taker Norval stopped Jaques' mouth with his hand before he could get anything unmentionable out.

"We can't find them, your Majesty," said the executioner.

"Nonsense!" replied the king; "Darwin has put it in a book, and therefore there must be. Besides, the Family Herald has lots of tales; and what a Family Herald has, surely a Royal Herald can have too!"

At last they found them—two very small swallow tails indeed—one of which was duly chopped off, but the other spared, as the king had forgiven half the fault; and the executioner, taking his stand on the form used at Charles the 1st's execution, lifted up the tail and solemnly said, "This is the end of a cratur."

The herald looked very disconsolate, and the executioner, clapping him on the shoulder as he sat on the block, said to him—

"How do you feel now, old boy?"

"No thanks to you for axing; your chop's a very cruel kind of cut let's say no more about it."

"Pooh, my good fellow! you're not so badly off; you've one all right."

"No, I've one left—it's the right one that's gone."

"Well, well, but you don't need to have it left so; they'll right you at any retail place in no time."

"Enough of chops, and cutlets, and tails," suddenly shouted the king; "now for the royal stakes—is that course ready?"

"Yes, your Majesty," said the Secretary of

Steak; "the entries are just over, and so the beef-eaters can come on now." They soon got through the removes necessary, and the game course cleared; whereupon the king's and queen's suites were set in their places, including the cream of society, and a following which was quite the cheese.

"Now," said the king, "every man shall have his desert. Go on with the heats,"—heats being apparently the Blunderland substitute for ices.

This injunction made the officials warm to their work, so that all was quickly ready, and the competitors came running up to take their places. They were a funny-looking set altogether. There was a fast young gentleman, who looked as if he had not been in bed all night, but had just come out of a bandbox. There was a scarlet-runner, who was the pink of condition; a post-runner, who of course was clad in a mail suit; a fore-runner, who went sometimes on his fore legs, and sometimes on his four legs; and an old woman, who said she would warrant her tongue to go faster, and to run on longer, than anybody on the ground. A solemn discussion arose among the judges, upon the question whether a tongue could be allowed to enter for the race; and it was at last decided that it must not, as the race was a

flat one, while the old woman's tongue was more than usually sharp.

The aged dame was very angry at this, her much-despised member going on at such a rate, that she, when told to hold it, excused herself on the ground that it was going too fast to be caught up without a stretch of imagination, which, at her age, was quite beyond her powers. So, as her tongue could not be stopped, the police took a homœopathic process, and simply ordered her and the offender to " move on ; " whereupon, with female contradiction, she did the very opposite, and moved off.

" That woman's tongue is equal to any two," said the clerk of the course ; "so, if a couple more would like to come forward and take its place, they may do so."

Thus invited, Norval and Jaques stepped out. Their appearance, with their coils wound round them, was that of a pair of screws, and this led the other competitors to look on them with contempt, apparently thinking that such well-hooped casks could never run.

But the boys paid no attention to the sneers. They intended to run for the sport of it—to win if possible, and to take it cheerfully if they could not ; which is the proper spirit for all boys, young or old, when they are going in for a contest.

On the start taking place, the fore-runner was soon left behind, the post-runner found his mail suit rather heavy, the scarlet-runner proved to be only a creeper, and there were none left except the fast young man and the two boys. At first Norval and Jaques with their young legs got a good start, as the fast youth, not having been in bed, had forgotten to wind up his watch, and being unaccustomed to get on without tick, had to stop till he got it wound. But as the race was a long one, he soon made up for lost time, and it looked as if the boys would get the worst of it, for at the third round of the course, Jaques was many yards behind, and his brother also losing ground; when, to the surprise of everybody, Norval suddenly shouted " Neck or nothing !" uncoiled his neck, and collared his opponent by shooting it out to the winning-post. This feat was received with deafening cheers, which were redoubled when Jaques, taking the hint, threw his long arms out over the head of the fast young man, and vaulting on his hands, flew over him, far past the winning-post, and got in a second before him.

The fast young man lodged a pro-

test, maintaining, in a style even louder than the style of his trousers, that Norval had won by neck-romantic arts; and that Jaques, instead of going on foot, had taken a fly, and so cabalistically over-reached him by craft. After the judges had looked very wise for ever so long—in fact, as long as Norval's neck itself—they decided that the neck being a neck, it did not matter whether it was romantic or not; and as it could not be alleged that Jaques had used any other craft than handicraft, his using feats of arms for feats of feet was quite allowable, he having only availed himself of his own handy capacity; and that as to his taking a fly, it was not a handsome thing to call it cabalistic, and an argument that only a for weal or woe begone growler would think it fair to take his hackneyed stand on. Norval was therefore declared first, and Jaques second, amid loud applause; and the fast young man, with his views dissipated, went off a bad third.

The next race was a blindfold one. The competitors having their eyes tied up at the winning-post, were led back to the scratch, and started; the rule being that, if any one wandered to the side of the course and fouled the ropes, or went beyond the post without touching it, he was out of the race. Now Ranulf, who came forward to run, kept wondering to himself what he should do to win.

"You see," he said, speaking to himself, "I've not got anything but a nose; and how can a long nose help me to see? and it's the blindfolding that is the bother. If I only had an eye at the tip, that would be jolly, only it wouldn't be fair not to tell them to tie it up too. What *am* I to do?"

Now Ranulf had still some of Victoria's sweetmeats in his pocket, and Ranulf was a boy; so it fell out that when he felt perplexed and did not know where to turn, he, as a matter of course, thrust his hands into his pockets, and it followed naturally that the sweetmeats got into his hand, and that his hand set off on a journey to his mouth. They had a most delicious perfume, so strong that though Ranulf's nose was wound round him so many times, the scent got through it into his head in a jiffy, or rather in a sniffy. The moment this happened, he began to rub his head very hard, as if something had struck him. He was struck, as it so happened; and

although it was only by an idea, it had got so
firmly into his head that it must have struck
him pretty forcibly. He immediately set himself
to work it out. When the competitors were ready
to start, Ranulf shot his nose out up the course,
sniffing for the first thing he had noticed lying on
the side of it that could be discovered by smel-
ling. It looked so funny to see this projection
waving about, like some dozens of those long
wooden serpents that they have at the toy-shops
put end to end, that the whole crowd set up a
tremendous shout of laughter. One man, however, did not seem to like it at all. He was the
backer of another competitor, and rushed up in a
very forward manner (particularly for a backer),
shouting—

" I object; it's not fair!"

Upon this the umpires were at once summoned;
and after being told what the matter was, one of
them addressed the backer, and said—

" We understand you have some objection to

o

this gentleman's nose; state your proposition." *

" He's got his nose out in front of him; it's not the correct tip."

The referees again looked very wise, pursing up their mouths, as if the words that were to come from them were gold; and after comparing notes, one of them solemnly said—

"While it seems to the referees that it is scarcely their province to sit upon long noses, these not being matters of course, we think we are justified in holding that a gentleman who wishes to follow his own nose, and trust to his own tip, instead of getting a tip from anybody else, is entitled to do so."

The backer at this got very excited, and shouted, " Nay, nay, but you surely won't go so far——"

" Sir," said the referee, sternly, "this is a foot-race, so you need not mount your high horse,

* In the original MS., this word was written proboscition by the author in his innocence.—ED.

neighing at us in that way. The referees have
carefully considered the length of the gentleman's
nose, and, long as it is, their opinion goes that
length. So let there be an end of it."

The backer, seeing he could make nothing of
it, marched off, muttering, " End of it, indeed !
it's *no* end of a nose that fellow's got. There's
one comfort, it can't be called a straight tip."

All this wrangling had served Ranulf's purpose, for it gave him time to con over his lesson.
And a very funny lesson it was. He had observed all the smelly things on the sides of the
course that the people in taking their refresh-
ments had thrown on the grass inside the ropes ;
so his lesson went thus :—

Right side,	. .	Peppermint-drop.
Left side,	. .	Ginger-beer bottle.
Right side,	. .	Cigar-end.
Left side,	. .	Skin of onion.
Right side,	. .	Orange-peel.
Left side,	. .	Nosegay.

The winning-post was opposite the place where the ladies and gentlemen sat, and of course they did not throw orange-peel, or anything of that kind, about. Ranulf had been greatly puzzled how to find his way there; but, luckily, a lady had put a splendid nosegay on one of the posts, and Ranulf, in going forward to be blindfolded, had a good sniff of it, so that he was sure he would find it all right.

At last the race began, and a very queer business it was; for the runners, in trying to avoid coming against the ropes, wandered about in the most extraordinary fashion. But Ranulf's performance was quite irresistible, and it would have cured the worst fit of sulks in all the world just to see him for a minute, stretching out his nose, and working it from side to side, like an elephant's trunk. He first found the peppermint-drop, up to which he rushed, winding up his nose on the ground like a coil of rope in a ship, then throwing it out again he found the ginger-beer bottle, and so on. He was rather put out by coming upon

orange-peel just after passing the cigar-end; and
when this happened, the puzzled look of his nose,
as it caught scent of the peel at the wrong place,
made the crowd roar again. The truth was, that
some one in the crowd was throwing orange-peel;
but, fortunately, a piece hit him on the nose, so
that he guessed what was wrong, and with a bold
sweep caught scent of the onion-skin from afar,
and on he went, winning easily by a nose. The
ladies were so delighted with this performance,
that they all wanted to kiss him at once, and
for a couple of minutes his nose was in great
requisition.

In the distribution of prizes, Norval was made
merry as a cricket by the gift of a golden bat;
Jaques being declared entitled to an armful of
toys, was able to claim enough to fill a bazaar by
the aid of his long arms; and Ranulf, whose
greatest delight was horses, rejoiced in a real
Lilliputian pony of 25 pounds, the proper figure
for a pony gained at races. When the prize
distribution was over, the boys were led to the

king's table, on which an elegant feast was spread.

While they were enjoying it, there was a sudden flutter, and every eye turned one way.

"Oh, here he comes! here's Blunderbore!" was the cry that rose on all sides.

"Blunderbore?" said Ranulf, turning rather pale; "that's the giant with the awful teeth and the big club. I thought Jack had killed him. Oh dear, what shall we do?"

Norval did not feel quite comfortable either, but, seeing little Ranulf's pale face, he forgot himself, and, trying to cheer him, said as bravely as he could—

"Never mind, Ranny; you know with my long neck I can make myself as big as he is, and I will brandish my bat as a club—perhaps that will frighten him." He was not very confident of this, but put on as much appearance of being at ease as he could, so as to encourage his little brother.

"It's Jaques' business to kill him," said Ranulf,

solemnly. " It's a good thing he has got long enough arms."

Jaques did not seem to see it, and the whole three were anything but comfortable in their minds.

It was somewhat reassuring, however, to notice that the news of the arrival of Blunderbore appeared to distress none of the rest of the company. The ladies were all looking through their opera-glasses, with faces which showed that he had no terrors for them. The gentlemen seemed, on the whole, to be rather disgusted, as the announcement of the giant's approach appeared to throw them entirely into the shade so far as the fair sex were concerned, and they looked at one another with glances of pique and contempt, as the ladies twittered away in eager conversation—eyes sparkling, lips smiling, and that curious buzz that always heralds a great arrival running through the whole assemblage.

" Any room for me?" said a voice (which, though evidently kept as mild as possible, made a sound very like the Westminster chimes striking the first quarter), as a face about three yards long, below a three-cornered cocked-hat, made its appearance under the fern-leaf fringe of the tent of flowers. Blunderbore had been compelled to stoop down so low in order to look in that his face was level with his knees, and as it was very round, the effect was ludicrously like a circular clock on pillars. The moment the face became visible, all strange and unpleasant thoughts began to fade from the boys' minds, for it was the picture of jolly good-nature. His eyes, the balls of which were larger than a Christmas plum-pudding, fastened themselves specially on Ranulf, and putting out a vast hand, he shook a forefinger as large as a bolster at him, saying—

"Now, I know you are expecting me to say Fe-fo-fum, something about grinding bones, and all that."

"Y-e-e-e-e-s, sir," said Ranulf, half frightened, but only half; for the jolly face was so good-humoured that it was almost impossible to be afraid.

" Well," said Blunderbore, taking him up on
his vast hand, " giants in Blunderland don't talk

rubbish of that kind, and they are not such geese
as to grind bones when they want to make bread."

" Come in, Blunderbore; we will make room
for you," came in a surging ripple from hundreds
of fair lips, while, with many a rustle of silk and
velvet, they cleared a large space on one side of
the amphitheatre, the seats of which rose in tiers
one above the other.

" Well, but your ceiling is so low.   However,

perhaps old Blunderbore can cure that for you,"
said the giant, as, pushing his head in below the
ombrelle of flowers, he placed his forefinger in
the centre of the white lily at the top, and, apparently without an effort, raised the canopy aloft.
Showers of diamond drops fell thick and fast
from between the fern-leaves as the gorgeous
ceiling rose, faster and ever faster, till at every
leaf there stood a glassy pillar, glittering and
sparkling with wondrous lustre, and in a twinkling
the bower became a crystal floral palace, to which
that of Covent Garden is but a dingy, dull, de-
pressing dungeon. Blunderbore then made his
way through the crowd with great care, of which
there was much need, his feet being nearly as big
as the dingies of a ship of the line, and seated
himself on the side of the hall that had been
vacated for his accommodation. He certainly
was very unlike the old kind of Blunderbore, from
the top of his three-cornered hat down to the
red heels of his buckled shoes. A magnificent
single-breasted coat and long flap-waistcoat, with

golden stripes, separated by lines of rich maroon-
coloured velvet, took the place of the short arm-
less blouse, and the great belt with a buckle like
a wicket-gate, that are supposed generally to be
the orthodox costume of gentlemen more than
eight feet high. And instead of the gnarled club
or grievous crab-tree cudgel of the story-books,
our Blunderbore carried a most elegant cane with
a golden top. It is true that the cane was as
thick as an ordinary lamp-post, but still it looked
quite neat and tiny, appearing slight enough in
Blunderbore's vast hand to suit the most foppish
taste. His breeches were of yellow satin, below
which were stockings of silk of the same colour,
and his curly hair was of a golden tint. Altogether, he made a most presentable-looking giant,
and seemed to be a special favourite with the
ladies, to whom, as he sat down, he kissed his
hand right gallantly. This done, he produced
from his waistcoat-pocket a snuff-box, larger than
a full-sized trunk, and took a pinch out of it, giving
his hand an elegant shake—in fact, quite *à la* Cox-

comme il faut of the last century, sending a shower
of snuff from his fingers like the stream from the
rose of a watering-pot.   This, the boys expected,
would set every one sneezing ; but such snuff was
not likely to get into any one's nostril by accident,
the particles being as large as ordinary peas, and
no one seemed inclined intentionally to make his
nose a *pis aller* for what the giant threw away.
As what remained between his fingers would have
stuffed an ordinary pillow, it proved that Blunderbore was anything but a bad fellow at a pinch,
and completely allayed the fears of our little men,
so that they were not the least alarmed when he
gave a terrific sneeze, like a squall of a north-
easterly gale—a perfect Blunder Boreas.

"Now, then," said he, "what can I do to pro-
mote the harmony of the meeting ?"

"Give us some music ; let's have a Monstre
Concert," was the cry that rose on every side.

"All right," said Blunderbore ; "will you have
the Jolly Waggoner ?"

"No, no! no Wagner, please ; we don't want

the music of the future; no promissory notes for us.*

"Well, I daresay you are right," replied Blunderbore; "the music of the future is no pastime. What do you say to a present of Chopin Morceaux ?"

"The very thing," arose in a shout of delight from every side.

"All right, then; here goes," said the giant; "and I am sure you will admit that I give you admirable concerted pieces."

The ladies seemed to know what was going to happen, for about 6o of them at once clustered round Blunderbore.

"Are you ready ?" said the giant.

"Yes," rippled in feminine tones all around him.

Blunderbore at once stiffened up, in a manner that formed a marked contrast to his previous

* Boys should take this as one of their mottoes—"No bills or promissory notes for us." There are too many sharps ready to press them on young naturals and flats, and they very often end in harsh keys and gloomy bars.—ED.

easy affability, squared at the whole company, and displayed any amount of brass. It soon appeared, however, that, just like a great many other people when asked to give a little music, he was making a fuss about the preliminaries, for presently, when he had looked stuck-up for a minute or two, he executed a most elegant breakdown, ending in a thoroughly organic change and brilliant musical parts, which latter the ladies caught neatly as they fell, and there, in a moment, stood a full orchestra, with a monster organ in the middle, as Blunderbore's gold-striped coat and waistcoat became gilded pipes, his curly locks fell in a shower of cornets and French horns, his stock made a full-sized drum, his cuffs a couple of brass drums, his cheeks a pair of cymbals, the bones of his nose naturally became a group of trombones; the fingers and nails scattering in a shower of violins, flutes, piccolos, clarionets, and oboes, and the thumbs in violas and bassoons; his arms making a splendid set of sax-horns, euphonions, and ophicleides; the legs forming two enormous double basses, and his

feet dividing into two pairs of violoncellos; while
the pin at his breast dropped down as a neat jewel-
mounted conducting-baton, the cane bent itself
into a magnificent harp; and, to crown all, his hat
settled on the top of the organ, forming an elegant
carved screen over it. Tap, tap, went the baton
in the lovely hand of the conductress, as the
gentlemen formed themselves into animated music-
desks, which, in the case of the ladies who held
the different classes of violins, reversed the usual
saying, by giving them two bows to their strings.
Wave, wave, wave, swept the baton—one, two,
three, and off they went in a grand overture, the
fair performers playing their parts (of Blunderbore) to perfection. The lady with the harp was
the only disconcerted one, for, unfortunately,
Blunderbore had lost the cords and tassels
of his walking-cane, so when formed into a harp
the instrument was stringless, and the lady holding it, who had a solo to play, was in despair.
Ranulf, seeing her distress, mounted the orchestra,
saying, as he looked and fumbled among the con-

fused mass that forms the proper contents of a boy's pocket, "Here is something that will perhaps do." The lady, seeing the coils over his shoulder, misunderstood him; and there being no time to lose, she, in the very act of saying, "Thank you, dear," slipped his nose off his shoulder, and before he had time to know what was to happen, strung it on the harp, up and down, up and down, just as the conductress turned towards her to indicate the time for her solo. Her nimble feminine fingers were so gentle that Ranulf was not at all put out, and there was little time to think, for the beautiful arms were stretched out, the taper-fingers gave a rapid wave, and the harp poured out its richest notes, so that all stood listening entranced, as the graceful fingers made it speak, now in round rolling roughness, like the storm; now in rich fulness of music; and now in gentle brilliant trills, like the birds in a distant wood. Ranulf himself, who had a good ear, drank in the sweet sounds with eager delight, wondering as nothing since he left home had made him

P

wonder.   But, in an evil moment, forgetting his
good manners, which forbid speaking when a solo
is going on, he exclaimed—

" Oh, how awfully jolly ! "
Terrible was the result.   Everybody knows
how horrid the sound is when a person speaks
holding his nose ; but then he only grasps it at one
place.   Now Ranulf's, of course, was held at about

a hundred places on the harp, and so it sounded
100 times over the fearful twang, making everybody put hands to ears; and the lady harpist,
whose sweetest notes had been made so false as
to turn her harp into a lyre, was so struck that
she looked despair as black as blue eyes could.

Instantly, an indignant but good-natured cry
burst forth from the ladies of the orchestra, as they
turned upon Ranulf and sang *—

> You've made a pretty mess, Sir Nose;
>   Why did you try to chatter?
> A check you give to all our bows,
>   Our notes of hand you scatter;
> Our organ's drown-ed in a C
>   From nasal organ vile,
> Which now by us shall punished be
>   In most pertickler style.

And so it was; for all the ladies that were immediately round the harp, arming themselves
with feathers from their hair, or flowers from their
bouquets, rushed off in a chorus and down upon
Ranulf, to tickle his long nose, singing—

* *Air*—" I'll strike you with a feather."

Little rogue, ha ! ha ! I'll make you pay
  The false notes you have forced on us in this offensive
      way.
    I'll strike you with a feather,
    I'll stab you with a rose,
For making of our harp a liar,
By talking through the nose.

And, suiting the action to the utterance, the feathers and the roses were thrust forward in a score
of dainty hands to tickle poor Ranulf's offending
organ. But the lady who had strung him on her
harp, though she was shocked at the nasal twang
he had brought out of her and his instruments
combined, did not forget the aid he had given
when she was in a difficulty ; so, as the merry
group came to the attack, taking Ranulf up in her
arms, she seated him on the very top of the harp
out of reach (where, though not gilded, and in
knickerbockers, he did very well for a Cupid), and
did all in her power to protect him from the
thrusts of the feathers and roses. She succeeded
pretty well while only her own sex were engaged,
for, being a harpist, she could move her hands
rapidly over the strings and wave off the attack in

all directions. But what was Ranulf's horror to
see Norval and Jaques, like a pair of rogues as
they were, unable to resist the temptation to join
the fun, thrust their long neck and arms over the
bevy of fair ladies who surrounded him—Norval
with a rose in his mouth, and Jaques with a
feather in his hand. Ranulf knew at once that
he must go off into fits, for the lady could not protect him from the wild flights of the long neck and
hands as they flew about tickling his poor nose in
all directions. He resigned himself to his fate,
slid down to the ground, and went off in screams
of laughter, while the merry chorus round him
sang—

> Lazy dog, ha! ha! wake up, I say,
>   You surely don't intend to sleep upon the rug all day.
>   I'll strike you with a feather,
>   I'll stab you with a rose,
>   Unless you stop that horrid snore,
>   That's groaning through your nose.

And as he lay, the arms were still out to protect
him, only, instead of their being uncovered except
by handsome bracelets at the wrist, they seemed

to get grown over with something very like brown
merino ; and when a voice spoke, saying, "Now,
boys, leave him alone, will you ?—stop tickling

him at once," it was that of his nurse (for whom
his pet name, appropriately, was Harpin) ; and

there he lay, sprawling on his back on the rug, as she kept his brothers off him.

" But where's my nose ? " he exclaimed, as on putting up his hand to his tickled face he found that his coils were gone.

This question was received with a shout of laughter, in which Harpin joined, and Ranulf awoke to the fact that he had been dreaming.

But although he has returned from Blunder-land, leaving behind him his long nose, he has brought a pretty long tail home with him instead of it; and now, as he was often taught never to be a tale-bearer, it has been carried to the Black woods, and hid away in these leaves, in the hope that it may amuse other little people who chance to unfold it.

THE END.

www.ingramcontent.com/pod-product-compliance
Lightning Source LLC
Chambersburg PA
CBHW022000050726
47498CB00006BA/2161